aloha friends

OUTRAGE

BY

K. IMUS

enjoy —

K. Imus

Maui '02

DEDICATION

TO THIS MAGNIFICENT LAND

Library Of Congress Control Number
00-133719

OUTRAGE
ISBN # 0-9653584-3-7

Edited by: Lynn Kent

To obtain copies of other books by K. Imus,
Contact your local bookstore, library, or write to:
Keico Publishing Company
407 NW 132nd street
Seattle, WA 98177
Fax: 206-361-6249
E-mail: keithimus@aol.com
Send $ 3 to cover postage.
If you reside in Washington State, please send 8.6% State sales tax.

GALWAY The making of a gunfighter	$8.95
CHEYENNE WILLIAMS	$6.95
OUTRAGE	$6.95
ZERO SMITH	$6.95

PROLOGUE

Cheyenne Williams was a rascal and an opportunist who spent most of his time seeking pleasure of one kind or another. He liked to fight, drink whiskey, gamble and get laid, probably in the reverse order. Williams was a “mixed blood” and had the best of it all. He was an Adonis who was part Indian, white, black and Hawaiian. He was tall, muscular, handsome and hung. The guy was all man.

Women liked him and they would lie down for him like wheat in front of a scythe. Two problems: many of them had husbands, and Cheyenne’s scruples were nearly nonexistent. If the woman was willing, that’s all that mattered. If an offended husband mentioned pistols at dawn, Cheyenne just beat the hell out of him right there on the spot. If the man wore a gun, he usually broke the fellow’s trigger finger as a little added insurance. If the husband had the reputation of a “pistolero,” then he cut the man's trigger finger off, on both hands if he was a two gun.

Cheyenne was first and foremost a survivor; with his enemies he was ruthless. He was also probably the world's best knife thrower and a dead shot. His grandfather, who learned knife throwing from a French trapper, taught Cheyenne this important skill, starting when Cheyenne was a small boy. At fourteen, he was an expert. His wise grandfather said, "Guns often misfired," which was particularly true in his grandfather's day. "They are noisy, and they give your position away to your enemies, but knives are always as good as your skill and they are silent."

Knife throwing among the Indians was almost unknown. There were several reasons for this. It took a long time to make a knife, and it was a treasured item. It also took a long time to learn the skill of throwing a knife and there was a great risk of breaking or losing it. Among the Indians, arrows took the place of knife throwing. Arrows were silent killers and they were accurate from a greater distance. They were also easier to make. Every man had a knife, but he rarely let go of it. Obsidian was the material most often used for making the blades. It was sharp, but very brittle. If thrown, one was very likely to have a handle and a lot of small pieces of obsidian. Cheyenne Williams got around this problem by trading for or buying steel knives when he was in the white-man's village.

Cheyenne Williams usually had the look of a buckskin-clad plainsman, but he sometimes dressed in city clothes. He liked the life the better hotels offered: the good whiskey, the food, and, of course, the ladies. Money was never a problem. Cheyenne lived well wherever he was, and he was always well armed. He was extremely well armed!

At the moment, he was armed with three knives and behind his most unusual, large, elk-horn buckle he carried a double-barreled Derringer .44. He wore a dark, flat crowned, wide brimmed, leather hat that was as tough as a dried buffalo hide shield. He was wearing a buckskin shirt and pants, and high Apache moccasins with a throwing knife in each one. He had an elk-hide gun belt of his own design that carried a huge knife and his Colt .44 revolver. In addition to all of that, he had two .44 Colt saddle pistols and a Winchester. When necessary he also had several pre-loaded revolver cylinders ready to replace the one in his pistol.

When Cheyenne once said,

"I liked to be prepared."

His friend Todd of the Zero Ranch had said,

"Prepared, Hell, you're more than prepared. You're a walking arsenal."

Cheyenne Williams could hit a playing card at forty feet with any of his knives and the corner numbers on a card at thirty feet. He could also shoot a hole in a thrown double eagle coin with either hand.

Williams was raised and educated in both the Cheyenne Indian culture, and the whiteman's culture. He went back and forth between cultures, from tepee lodges to houses, and back to lodges again until he was about fifteen.

Soon after, in a white orphanage school, he met an attractive young blonde teacher with a body to die for. He met the insatiable Miss Moresby.

She taught him a variety of skills, some of which came under the heading of academics. One of these skills was reading the classics. He read Shelley, Keats, Coleridge and Moresby. Then he read some American writers such as Washington Irving, Poe, Emerson, Thoreau, Whitman, particularly his Leaves of Grass, and of course, some more Moresby.

He read a whole lot of Moresby. The superficial scratches on his back, put there by the exuberant Miss Moresby, were what she called "marks of valor." The marks were a nuisance, but he was sure they were worth it. Her "sexuberant squeals" [his word] of delight, raised some eyebrows in the hallowed halls of education, but they were never actually caught in the act, an act that was very nearly an infinite continuum while he was there. A fundamental tenet of the "Moresby School" proclaimed a strong belief in "repetitive learning." One, or in this case two, must spend considerable time trying to get it right.

His enthusiasm for learning extended toward the academic as well. Probably, because Miss Moresby required lots of home work,

Cheyenne Williams became a reasonably well-educated young man in the usual areas, and superbly well educated in the area he cared most about. He was already a serious hedonist, but Miss Moresby had put the icing on his hedonistic cake. A year and a half later, when the young Adonis left the orphanage, he was sure he had attended one of the better schools of learning, and the insatiable Miss Moresby had a tear in her eye.

//////

For the next several years, Cheyenne Williams would slide in and out of both the white man's world, and the Indian's world, with the ease of an otter going into the water. He would occasionally return to slide into the world of Miss Moresby as well, much to her delight.

He continued to drift from a village of lodges to a village of houses and back again depending on whose toes he had stepped upon and more specifically, depending on the woman he was with. If he was with an Indian maiden, there were no problems unless she was married. If the woman was Indian and married and she was caught in an act of infidelity, she risked having the end of her nose cut off by her husband. Conversely, her husband risked having his life cut off if he even thought of doing such a thing to a woman Cheyenne Williams cared about.

Williams' reputation as a dangerous fighting man was awesome. He was a warrior of major status among most of the plains tribes. He had fought for several different tribes at one time or another, but was equally renowned among the tribes he had fought against.

The enemy had a tendency to make war at the drop of a loincloth. Occasionally, it happened when Cheyenne was in the lodge of an eager damsel. He was furious with the fools who had nothing better to do than look for scalps, so he did what he could to bring those small wars to an end as soon as possible. His was a major contribution. He usually killed three or four times as many of the enemy as any of the other warriors. There were two very good reasons for this. He had more and better weapons and he didn't waste time taking scalps.

Cheyenne's anger and his weaponry were a powerful combination. He had a low flash point and a high anger that would terrify a grizzly bear. In battle, the man was a formidable warrior. His physical strength was phenomenal and his staying power, relentless. Women facetiously said the same thing about him when he was in their beds. Apparently he was formidable in several areas.

CHAPTER ONE

MEXICO

Cheyenne Williams left the whorehouse because he was nearly broke. He was feeling like death and was getting signals from Hell of an approaching gigantic hangover and the dreadful nauseating feeling that usually went with a ten-day drunk. He was saying his atheistic prayers to anyone else's gods who would allow him to sleep until the pounding in his head went away. He'd felt like this before, not often, but more than once.

Cheyenne had tied his hammock in the shade between two posts, which held up the awning in front of what, in Old Mexico, passed for the local general store. Watching these proceedings, the little merchant became slightly unhinged and began to tremble. It was his customary reaction to any kind of problem. Cheyenne Williams was not the sort of man one approached without some trepidation. The little man looked intently at Cheyenne and just knew that the big gringo was a problem of major proportions. This was truer than he realized. He looked warily into his own smart box and shrewdly decided to leave well enough alone.

Cheyenne had chosen the only adequate shade on the square of this small Mexican town. There were other awnings in town, but none with posts stout enough to support the weight of a powerful six foot two inch, rough cob like Cheyenne Williams.

Williams always did pretty much as he pleased and now he was borrowing the little man's shade to have a snooze. He rationalized that the merchant would be glad to have him there, as word was out that he was a spender. He thought it unlikely that the merchant would be disturbed by his presence. In reality, the situation was quite the contrary. The presence of Cheyenne that close to his store had scared the hell out of the little fellow.

As if that weren't enough, that very afternoon, while Cheyenne was peacefully dozing away, the merchant was robbed, by two of the local bandits.

Biiiiiiiggg mistake!

If they had been quiet about it, Cheyenne would not have cared about the little man's problems, but they fired their pistols to scare everybody during their escape and deliberately killed an old man who had accidentally happened upon the scene. The loud noise woke our very disgruntled hero in time to see the old fellow fall.

To Cheyenne, suffering the effects of a dreadful hangover, the gunshots were like knives through his brain. He was more than a little perturbed, and from his hammock he threw two knives, one at each bandit to put their lights out. He very angrily retrieved his knives from each corpse, cleaned the blades on their shirts and went back to his hammock to sleep. The two bandits had mistakenly assumed that he was just another Mexican peasant sleeping away the afternoon heat. Wrong! It was very poor reasoning on their part and they would have eternity to contemplate their poor judgment. Where Cheyenne Williams was concerned, one should never make assumptions.

A couple of hours later, the little merchant was a basket case. Who wouldn't be, with two stiffs lying around gathering flies, and a killer sleeping soundly in the shade right there in front of his store? It was enough to drive a man to drink and it was certainly bad for business. Besides, he couldn't make change unless he went through the pockets of the dead outlaws. That thought rattled him even more. No, he was not about to do that.

An hour later, Cheyenne, finally awake, noticed the little man was coming apart, and suggested a touch of the sauce for each of them. The speechless merchant nodded, stumbled to oblige, and was finally settled down by several stiff jolts of his own rather good tequila, diligently urged upon him by one of the world's more serious students of distilled anything. The terrified little merchant reasoned, "Who was he to refuse?" This was the line of defense he was already preparing to present to his wife. The woman, a round, deceptive looking little dumpling, was generally considered to be one of the "greater dragons" of this, or any other part of Mexico.

Later the little man did get up enough nerve to ask Cheyenne to retrieve the stolen loot from the pockets of the dead outlaws.

//////

Fortunately for Cheyenne Williams, the only local law was absent at the time. The local law was capriciously administered by the Military, the Federales. They were more of a threat to the citizens than protectors. They rode through every few weeks to rip off the locals.

Cheyenne was in old Mexico lying low after riding high with the "tinker bell" wife of a rich and irate rancher type in El Paso. The man had big political clout and a little tiny dick. He also had an army of cowhands riding for his brand. Large groups of unthinking men, who were armed and dangerous, always made Cheyenne Williams a little nervous. It was one thing to deal with a husband, but quite another to deal with a husband who led an army of "kill for the brand" cowboys.

Williams had stopped in El Paso, a dubious burg at the time, long enough to get laid. He had gallantly agreed to rescue the fair damsel and afterward she had been more than convinced he had. Both parties had enthusiastically ignored her marital vows with equal diligence and their romp had turned into one of heroic proportions.

"You certainly did come to my rescue," she said, smiling.

"Yes." He grinned, enjoying the double meaning. "And you to mine, several times."

"To be more accurate in my case, countless times," she giggled.

Afterward, they were both wrung out. Cheyenne's back was marked with a few new scratches, but his handsome face wore the big dumb grin of a Cheshire cat. "Tinker bell" also wore a big dumb grin on her face, but walked rather carefully at times for the next several days.

Getting laid was Cheyenne's primary reason for stopping in El Paso, but then, it was his primary reason for stopping anywhere. It was also his primary reason for going on to anywhere. Others argued for the work ethic, power, wealth, religion, ranching, mining, warfare, etc. but Cheyenne Williams was never convinced. In fact, he thought it would be difficult to make a positive case for most human endeavor. He very much intended to continue to pursue his life of pleasure with the ladies. He was a true hedonist and one of an elite group of the most selfish men alive. He was convinced his form of hedonism was a holy mission and that he had been called to go among the flock and spread the word. "Word" in this case was another of his euphemisms. After all, someone had to do it!

Many men, throughout history, had been knighted for doing much the same thing. Cheyenne was not likely to be knighted for his endeavors unless it was vaguely related to "The Order Of The Garter." However, he did smile smugly upon occasion. He was convinced that he, and perhaps a few others, had in fact found his idea of the Holy Grail. At least he thought he knew where to look for it. He felt each new romp was another great challenge to be met, heroically, if possible. In some circles, he was considered a true champion, even an aficionado of the craft. He didn't care how he was considered, as long as it was often.

After a ten-day debauch that featured the best in sophisticated erotica via women and booze, and an incredible variety of both, Williams had managed to trash his head, his body, and all of his nerve endings. Now, at long last, our champion lay defeated by self-indulgence. He had a serious hangover and all the charm of an angry grizzly bear.

He should have worn a sign that said, "Danger, highly explosive."

On his best day he tended to over react, but on days when he felt this badly it was a mistake to be within miles of this muscular devil.

In lawless country Cheyenne Williams made his own law, and he did it better than anyone. The two bandits were simply unlucky. Perhaps if they had practiced their trade on a day when Cheyenne Williams was not around, they might have been more successful.

Meanwhile, Williams had more tequila. It was just hair of the dog. Cheyenne had sense enough to taper off slowly. In another ten days he would be his inordinately good looking and charming self to women, and as usual, a threatening menace to most men. Williams was convinced that the West had far too many men, anyway. When he applied his form of justice and took out the bad guys, he said, “Good riddance.”

Even if it was a husband, he called it “icing on the cake,” though he rarely seriously trashed the husbands. After all, he didn’t want their women permanently. He only wanted to borrow them for awhile, sometimes for several days. When he was gone, they would still need care and feeding until he came back the next time.

The day came when he was nearly broke and he planned to ride to his gold stash. On the way, he intended to visit an old friend who was a great chief of what was now a small band of the Cheyenne.

Williams had loafed his way through warm, lazy days in the Mexican sun long enough. A few days later, though still a little bent, he said “Good bye” to his several senoritas.

He paid his bill at the hotel, and he paid his damages in the bar. The damages amounted to some trashed furniture and a large window through which Cheyenne had tossed a man. He located his horse and also paid for the beast’s damages. It seems the big stud horse had trashed a board fence on his way to a long-lashed mare. The local was very pleased. He was paid now for his broken fence and would be paid again later with a quality foal. He watched our heroes, man and horse, ride off down the road, all three quite pleased with themselves. The senoritas and the mare were sorry to see them go.

//////

Cheyenne rode north at a fast, ground covering pace along a road that many days later just dissolved into an ocean of grass. He was riding his big Appaloosa stallion. The horse was a man killer and Williams had to warn people to stay away from him every time he went to a livery stable. The big horse didn't really like anyone. He tolerated Cheyenne probably because he just knew Cheyenne Williams would cut his heart out if he misbehaved. It seemed the nag had horse sense the way a wild creature often does. Either way it was not a good bet to cross Cheyenne Williams. It's likely he had never heard of the pet concept. Many western men regarded their horses as tools, or transportation, much like wagons or pistols. However, in Cheyenne's case, if the critter goofed, Cheyenne might have given him a second chance, depending on the severity of the breach of confidence.

The big horse was a great ride. He was smooth in all gaits, strong as a bull, swift as lightning, could run forever, and he was a damn good watchdog. The boss and the horse got along, because they each had respect for the other's nasty disposition. Cheyenne admitted the nag probably had more class than he did, because the horse was a pure bred and he was just a mongrel. Cheyenne did not demand a lot of respect from the horse, but he did like the critter to pay attention when he was around. One time he literally knocked the horse to his knees. He smacked him right between the eyes with his fist for showing Cheyenne too much disdain. From then on the big stud horse always paid attention. Just after the incident, Cheyenne quietly spoke to the horse in a Cheyenne dialect meant to clarify a simple philosophy for the great beast, something to the effect that his job was to be a plus in the life of one Cheyenne Williams, and any show of intolerable negatives would immediately get him killed and eaten.

These two had been a team long enough to have an understanding. His big horse was seventeen hands high, and Devil mean. The horse went where, when, and as fast as Cheyenne wanted him to, and Cheyenne prevented other people from killing the surly beast. The critter knew damn well that his role was to be a swiftly moving, battle platform for his boss. Cheyenne, with lance or ax and his many white-man weapons, protected the nag from the other warriors' weapons.

The charging big stud had literally knocked any number of smaller Indian ponies ass over bow and arrow. Cheyenne was never sure if the huge animal did it to look out for his boss, or just out of meanness. Several times the big brute bit hell out of the enemy on the way by. He had chewed on warriors several times and he had bitten their horses many, many times. On those occasions, Williams was rather proud of the big monster.

CHAPTER TWO

A capricious wind marked its various directions across the prairie by pushing wind-waves over the grass and the few early wild flowers. Overhead, the great white cotton-ball clouds followed a steadier path, herded northeast by a much higher invisible wind. It was a good time; winter had passed and the land was being reborn.

Williams was back in wide-open grassland that rolled well beyond the horizon. Many days ride later the vast grassland still went to the horizon. He was riding through an ocean of waving grass. He was in buffalo country and he liked it. There were new calves everywhere and game of all kinds. The hunters had not yet begun to decimate the vast herds and there was game for all. He traveled west toward the mountains, then turned north again to follow the rivers where possible. The huge herds were going the same way he was, but for slightly different reasons. They were filling their bellies with grass and he intended to fill his pockets with gold. Cheyenne Williams was broke, and he was returning to his own personal bank, his "glory hole." It was located in the mountains beyond the summer campsites of the Cheyenne People.

A few years back, while wintering with the Sioux, he was out hunting meat for a ripe and grateful widow, when Cheyenne was caught in a winter storm. The storm became much more severe than he anticipated. The wind blew the snow into massive swirls of white light. Visibility was down to zero and the temperature was way below that. He guessed it was about thirty below, with wild winds increasing by the minute. The driving swirls and deepening snow screamed at him to "find shelter or die out here." Fortunately for him and his horses, he stumbled onto shelter under a large, fallen cottonwood tree. The old tree had blown down over a small ravine and he sheltered in the space underneath, where the roots met the tree trunk.

Working furiously, but below a sweat, he cut and dragged tree limbs to build a lean-to that was large enough for him and his two horses. Then he built a fire. The driving snow piled up outside against the windbreak lean-to, and finally was thick enough to insulate his shelter from the terrible icy winds. The harder it snowed, the more snug, he became. With the fire burning well, and under his several buffalo robes, Cheyenne and the horses were bedded down in what amounted to bearable conditions under the circumstances. He reasoned they should all survive until morning. He hoped the vicious storm would pass on by then.

When it began to get dark, he noticed light from the fire being reflected back at him from several places in the tree roots. As night came on there were more and more of the shining spots; some close, some up higher. He clawed his way to the nearest one, dug it out with his knife, and returned to the fire to examine the acorn sized, hard, rough, shining shape. Sure enough, Cheyenne Williams had found gold, hundreds and hundreds of the little guys. He had found lots and lots of gold.

He was rich. He was richer than rich. He felt so good, he was ready to burst, but he didn't dare shout, so he laughed quietly, had a celebratory whisky and danced. He danced and he laughed, and then he danced some more. When he got tired of that, he rested. He took a more serious look at all of the reflections and began to carve away at the tree where the reflecting gold was imbedded. When he had dug a three-pound sack full of gold nuggets out of the tree roots, he realized he would be there for several days. Already his hands were tired and his knife was dull, a condition that would have been intolerable before tonight. He celebrated with some more whiskey and he dug more gold.

For the next few days he became a gold miner, or in this case, a gold gatherer. After cutting gold nuggets from the tree roots until his knives were dull and his hands were sore, he changed tasks. He made several small sacks from one of his old buffalo hides. Each seam had to be double stitched because the nuggets were so heavy. Most of the nuggets were about the size of his thumb from the end to the nearest joint; a few were even larger, and some were as small as a pea. There were a great variety of gold nuggets. Some were round, some were flat, some almond shaped, but all were rough nodules of pure gold. The old cottonwood tree had been guarding this golden stash for a hundred years. The gold itself, had been in this location for perhaps several thousand years, and for much of that time the gold may have been guarded by the ancestors of this same cottonwood tree. Perhaps that was the cottonwood tree's mission in life. The Cheyenne Indians believed that within each thing on the earth, there resided a life-spirit. Williams was neither pagan nor Christian, he was simply thankful that the "what ever spirit" chose this particular time to reveal the treasure to him. He vowed to be eternally grateful by having the best knives that money could buy. Otherwise, he would continue to live similar to the way he always had, but perhaps he wouldn't be quite so scruffy looking. On second thought, nah! He would be the same, but now he wouldn't have to take a job that he didn't want. Now he could ride for his own brand and drink a better quality of whiskey.

Like most Indians, Cheyenne wore a small sack on a thong around his neck. Theirs were filled with spiritual charms, - things they believed had good medicine, such as a small stone or a feather or piece of bone from a bird or animal, and the lot was carried for protection against evil spirits, but the small sack on a thong around Cheyenne's neck was filled with gold nuggets so he could buy spirits, and be protected from poverty.

Finally he had enough money to buy the best spirits that he believed in, to help him ward off the evil spirits that other people believed in; it was a great comfort to him. So was the thought that he would soon be among friends, spending time in their lodges and enjoying some of the women of the tribe.

Before he left his campsite, with the eye of an Indian, he carefully erased all signs that anyone had been there. He knocked down the lean-to and scattered the tree limbs. The ground was brushed with a tree limb, and the limbs, which had a fresh knife cut, were tied together to be dragged miles away. He even gathered and carried away all of the ashes from the fire pit, to also be scattered miles away. The still falling snow would cover over everything.

When he left he carried a light heart, enough gold to last him for a quite awhile, and he wore a big dumb happiness grin that lasted for several days. In the spring when the snow melted, there would be no gold above the ground for any chance visitor to find.

//////

Cheyenne Williams had lived with and fought for many tribes. He had fought mostly for the Cheyenne, of course, and secondly for several Sioux tribes: the Lakota, Dakota, the Brule, the Nakota and Hunkpapa Sioux. He had also fought for the Cree, the Shoshone, and even the Bannock on more than one occasion. He continued to fight for these people and against their enemies. Sometimes he fought out of a sense of duty or justice, or simply because he liked to fight. He had fought both for and against the Blackfeet, a condition most people understood. The Blackfeet were a quarrelsome lot.

He was a knight of the plains without any of the moral baggage of his medieval counterpart. Known as "Wims" to these people, Cheyenne Williams was considered a great warrior, and had been honored for his exploits in battle by most of these same tribes. A few tribes who were his known enemies had even honored Cheyenne Williams. Many of these enemies were marked in death, not by scalping, but rather, with his own personal calling card, the now famous "W" scar which stood for Wims. The W scar was drawn with the big knife by Cheyenne Williams, on some part of the chest or forehead of his dead enemies. Leaving the scalp intact allowed the dead warrior to join the Star People for all eternity. More important to Cheyenne, it would also tell anyone whom the victor was and any avenger whom to look for. It only took a few victims to establish who was doing the marking. The marks spread his reputation through the tribes with the speed of a grass fire and he took on all avenging challengers.

True, Cheyenne Williams did allow his dead enemy to keep his scalp, but to think it was altruism was to misjudge one of the world's most selfish men. Cheyenne Williams knew we all see the world through our own biased eyes. A dead enemy with his scalp still intact could take his spirit and his strength with him on his trip to the Star People, where he would be welcomed as a man who had not died in shame. For this reason many people of enemy tribes respected and were grateful to Cheyenne Williams. Yet, he had really marked his enemies to spread his own fame.

"Wims" had been a warrior for the Cheyenne People since he was fourteen, and he was now twenty-seven. He had been a fighting man for half of his life. The fact that he was still alive said a good deal about the man; so far, he had been the best.

//////

Cheyenne Williams was getting close to where he expected to reach the village of his good friends and blood brothers, the Cheyenne chief, Kua Tonta and his brother, Kicks Hard. They had all three been members of the elite Wolf Society within the Cheyenne tribe when they were in their teens. Each member had to take at least three scalps from the enemy of the Cheyenne to qualify for membership in the elite society of young warriors. Each of the three had sworn to avenge the death of the other two, if that situation ever occurred. During the ceremony each young man had been given a dream catcher to always have good "mistai," good ghost spirits, around them.

Cheyenne Williams was the youngest member ever to have been initiated into the illustrious Wolf Society. He was just fourteen, but his knives were deadly even then, and they were silent.

War was a way of life. Killing the tribe's enemies was how one gained status. Cheyenne Williams, being a half-breed, had many obstacles to circumvent. He wanted status more than most and he wanted it sooner than most. And he got it. At seventeen, he was a very respected warrior.

His exposure to the white man's world left him very skeptical about anyone's gods. He could not have cared less where his enemies went after they died. Wims welcomed all challenges in those days. Each vanquished enemy contributed to his awesome reputation and they felt honored, even in death, to have challenged such a great warrior. It was some years later that he began to mark his victims in battle with a large "W" scar.

//////

Back on the trail, he soon found where the village had wintered and followed it as the people moved north to another camp. There would be several such moves toward the higher country, before the hot mid-summer. The heavily laden travois left shallow grooves in the thick sod. The trod-upon wild flowers and broken stemmed grasses would recover. In time, it would seem as if only the "Mistai", the ghosts, had traveled here. After all, the miraculous grass withstood and recovered after the passing of a million buffalo, and oddly enough, was the better for it. Compared to that, the few villagers Cheyenne followed left hardly a mark on the land as they passed.

Four days later Cheyenne found the village, or what was left of it.

First, he saw the vultures circling. Then, even before he came to the village, he could smell it. It was the awful, rank, putrid, suffocating smell of death and destruction. Without looking, Cheyenne knew what he would find, but he expected the cause to be disease. He found the place decimated and with many dead, perhaps fifty. But it wasn't disease that had killed these people. It was fire and lead. They had all been lined up and shot: men, women and children, all ages and all dead. Their lodges and belongings had been burned and their horses run off. None of the men were holding weapons. There was nothing left but a horrible scar on the land and a worse scar on Cheyenne's memory. Even many of the ubiquitous dogs had been shot.

The village had apparently divided into three groups to follow the buffalo, which caused Kua Tonta's defense warriors to be few in number at the time of the raid.

Cheyenne studied the tracks left by the raiders. They had all ridden shod horses. The herd of Indian ponies they had stolen, probably as an after thought, looked to be about sixty. Cheyenne was sure this was the work of white men. The U. S. Army was raiding when they got the chance under a few generals, but this looked more like the work of renegades. The West was overrun with low-life predators. There were bands of hate-filled whackos, assorted thieves, murderers, deserters from the armies of both North and South, and outlaws of all kinds, all of them looking for gold, women, and anything of value. They crawled in their rabble numbers, over the lawless plains like locusts. They were shameless vermin feeding on the smallest opportunity. The West would never be a safe place to live, or to raise a family, until these lawless predators were all exterminated. Cheyenne Williams had long since vowed to do his part in cleaning up the country against evil men, Indian or white.

Cheyenne reasoned the village must have been taken by surprise, and the only way for this to have happened was through treachery. Kua Tonta was far too clever a chief to be ambushed by anyone. There were a few dead people scattered through the village, but most of them were murdered in one place. The chief's body and that of Kicks Hard were in that group. Their hands had been tied behind their backs before they had been shot.

Cheyenne Williams remembered his vow to Kua Tonta and Kicks Hard. Through clenched teeth, he spoke their names to the four winds. The wind would tell their spirits that he remembered his vow to find and destroy their killers. They would be avenged.

Cheyenne Williams was outraged. Suddenly, a large number of men were in a world of horribles, more than any of them could ever imagine. A few would find out what his big knife could do against their six guns.

//////

Williams made burial platforms for the bodies of his two friends, and supplied them with weapons for their journey to the Star People. As he worked, he repeated his vow to the winds, and to the four directions, to avenge the dead. He chanted his vow to the winds over and over. With each saying, his rage increased and was fueled by the rotting stench of death.

Cheyenne examined the destruction until he was sure he had all of the information he could get from the signs left by the raiders. He found a small triangular piece of blue cloth and one unusual horseshoe print in addition to the brass shells. There were spent cartridges everywhere. He picked up several cartridges of different calibers. Then he mounted and trailed the shod horses that had pushed the stolen Indian horse herd.

Just beyond the village on his way to his gold stash, Cheyenne found an unusual Colt .44. He dismounted and picked up the weapon. The bone grips had been hand carved into a bas-relief of a bull's head, with one horn on each side of the pistol grip. The artistry was very skillful and he judged the pistol to be quite valuable. Perhaps, someone would return to look for it. Now, Cheyenne rode Indian-cautious, and fox-careful, always expecting to meet a rider coming directly toward him.

The very next day, he did meet such a rider. The rider wore two holsters and one of them was empty. The man was looking at the ground, when he was suddenly halted by Cheyenne Williams.

The man looked up to see someone dressed as a plainsman. Plainsmen were generally a very salty group. It didn't do to take them lightly. The outlaw noted the darkly weathered buckskin outfit, the Apache style knee-high moccasins and the flat crowned hat. What he didn't notice was that Cheyenne was carrying his big knife in his hand. His throwing knives in his knee-high Apache moccasin-boots were at the moment, out of sight.

"Howdy."

Both men reined up their horses.

"Did you lose a pistol?"

"Yeah, but how did you know?"

"Well, it's your lucky day, because I found it. I was hoping you might give me some reward money for finding it for you."

"I guess I could do that," and with that, the man drew his other pistol and promptly fired it into the ground. Cheyenne had put the big knife in the fellow's gun arm shoulder when the man went for his gun. The huge blade severed a few tendons along the way. The rider dropped his gun, fainted, and toppled from his horse to the ground. Then Cheyenne Williams jumped down and landed with both feet on the man's chest, freeing some of the fellow's ribs from his sternum. The man would be even slower to heal, than he was to draw.

Williams waited for the man to come around, then whispered,

"Who was with you at the Cheyenne village?"

"Go to Hell."

"You are not listening. Who was with you at the village?"

The man groaned in great pain, but said nothing. Cheyenne put his foot against the man's chest and pulled the big knife out. The man fainted for a second time. Cheyenne poured water on his face and the man revived. The knife wound probably destroyed the use of his right arm for keeps, but he would live.

When the man opened his eyes, the first thing he saw was the huge knife and he was afraid. Then he saw the look of rage on Cheyenne's face and he was justifiably terrified.

Cheyenne put the point of his big knife back into the opening of the wound, still speaking in a whisper and demanded,

"Who was at the village?" He pushed the knife in just slightly, and the man screamed. He was suddenly ready to tell him anything: the names of the men, the names of their girl friends, the names of their horses, their dogs, anything at all.

Cheyenne made a list of those short lived people, nearly twenty in all, and said to the man,

"Is your name on here?"

"The first one."

"Who was the traitor who took out the night guards?"

"The breed, Frank Crow. He has a long crow feather on his hat."

"If the names are incorrect, I will be back to finish you off."

Cheyenne told him he was taking his guns and his horse, but leaving him food and water for a few days.

The man started to object.

"Just until I get back. Remember, I'm the only one who knows where you are. Stay here and rest, and the wound will heal. If you move around, you'll bleed out in an hour. Pray to your gods that I come back. If I don't make it, you probably won't either."

With that, Cheyenne turned his big stud horse and rode northwest, first to his gold, then toward the town of Warm Springs, so-called because of the active warm and hot springs around the area. It was rather like what was called the Yellowstone country, with the same geothermal forces at work and from the same source. Mother Nature periodically blew off a little steam around that area, to improve her disposition.

It also helped to keep the few locals on their toes. Some were sure the area was the devil's cauldron and when traveling nearby, vowed to clean up their acts in the future. Their resolve lasted as long as it took to ride through the area, after which, their "etched in stone resolve" usually vanished with the same speed it took a rental horse, that had dumped his rider, to return to his stable.

//////

The local wild life liked the varied temperature of the hot springs. The critters were sure the springs were designed by the Great Spirit for them to wallow in to keep warm during cold winter storms. Buffalo would sometimes lie in the warm spring water nearly submerged. When he saw them, Cheyenne thought the buffalo seemed to be smiling.

Cheyenne Williams was about to make war on a whole list of despicable people. They were "over" if he had his way, and he nearly always did have his way. The town of Warm Springs was close by, but he would take enough time to sharpen his knives and to hone his rage before he arrived.

When angered, Cheyenne Williams was not a nice man. Some said he didn't have a very firm grip on his emotions even on his best day, but when angered, he looked positively crazed. What he felt was more than mere anger. This feeling was a deep-seated rage that was part of his inner core. It was born in his ancient past and rumbled toward the surface each time he witnessed injustice, cruelty and inhumanity. This time, women and children had been lined up and shot. He was seething.

//////

Williams at one time was a fatherless boy, a breed, shunned by nearly every one, except his grandfather, who taught him the knife. At an early age, with the help of his extraordinary knife skill, he gained respect from his peers and even from adults. Ultimately, he grew into a great warrior, and eventually into a world-class survivor. Now years later, Cheyenne Williams was an enraged warrior who could read, a dangerous combination. He was a mature, experienced man, who was filled out, powerful and ruthless, and the killers of his friends were in deep trouble.

Riding through the country, Cheyenne was always alert to the signs of danger, but he also took time to appreciate the beauty of the area. Not this trip. He was all business, very alert, but he had little patience with Nature's reveries. Bird songs, the sounds of insects, and the sounds made by a meandering brook only registered in his sub-conscious. He was more in tune with the task ahead. If the men were all together, Cheyenne Williams was about to face what amounted to a small army. He was ready. If he didn't act he would explode from his own rage.

CHAPTER THREE

A few days travel brought him to Warm Springs, a sizeable cow town in a long, narrow valley in green plateau country. Cheyenne stopped at the aging livery stable and stabled his horse. He told the hostler,

"Keep everyone away from this big horse because he is a man killer. He's dangerous to anyone but me."

He went to the general store and bought a new file, some more ammunition, then proceeded to the nearest saloon for a drink. When he walked in, the locals were a little shaken by his awesome presence. The man looked lethal. When angered, he wore an aura of danger about him as another man might wear a coat. Cheyenne Williams was angry, very angry and he had built up a full head of steam. He sat down, sipped at his drink and began to sharpen his knives.

After a few moments, still sharpening his knives, he turned to face the locals and to ask if any of them knew of a man named Bradford. Cheyenne had already spotted the man named Crow sitting at a corner table with two other men. The crow's flight feather was visible on the crown of the man's hat. Cheyenne, looking directly at the man in the feathered hat, quietly asked,

"Do you know a man named Bradford?"

A tall gunman at the same table stood up, loosened the thong on the hammer of his pistol, and said,

"I'm Bradford."

"You helped massacre a Cheyenne village."

"What of it, I hate Indians and you're next."

Bradford's gun fired into the floor as Cheyenne's huge knife took him out. The other two men at the table went for their irons, and everyone else dived for cover.

Cheyenne Williams buried knives in the throats of the two men before they cleared leather. A fourth man at a far table was bringing up his shooter when Cheyenne shot him between the eyes. The big Colt splattered an assortment of horribles on some of the locals. Cheyenne had done all of this while he was still seated at the table. Now he stood up.

Cheyenne, appraising the room, grabbed one of the local men by his scrawny chicken neck, lifted the man with one hand until he stood on tiptoe, and said,

"Tell me the names of the dead men."

The man squawked,

"I, I, I only know two of them. Bradford, there, and Wills is that one across the room."

Cheyenne let go and the man collapsed in a heap on the saw-dusted floor. Williams, still pointing his pistol, faced about a dozen people.

"Everyone take a chair. Put your hands on the tables where I can see them. Now identify these other two dead men for me."

They readily obeyed. The two men were Crow, the traitor, which he already knew, and a known gunslinger named Forsythe. Forsythe's "gun for hire" days were over, but the outlaw shootist had friends. They were the boys Cheyenne Williams was looking for.

Every time he thought of the massacred village, of the slaughtered women and children, he got angry all over again. He was sure he would stay that way until all of the raiders were under. Even without thinking about it, he would be forceful and relentless. He would continue to distribute his own kind of justice in this lawless land. So far he was making a significant dent.

Most of these small western towns were too poor to afford a sheriff. Warm Springs was no exception. The locals were glad to be rid of these vermin and said so. They told Cheyenne the names of two more men who he put on the list.

They told him the two men frequented a grungy saloon just east of town. The place also served as the stagecoach line's reserve horse corral. The horses faired better than the people. The unpainted saloon was skillfully mismanaged by a very fat and sweaty, filthy slob. The atavistic proprietor, who hadn't bathed in years, specialized in neglect and sloth. He always wore a filthy and many-stained apron over his equally filthy bib-overalls for reasons that were not clear to anyone.

The saloon featured a long list of horribles: beater furniture, a much-cracked mirror behind the dirty bar, cheap rot-gut whisky and bad food, dead flies on the grungy window sills, and stained wall-paper that had long since faded to a neutral blah. Except for the wallpaper, it was a typical inn from the Dark Ages, but this guy was even too cheap and lazy to put cattail rushes on the floor. There were probably fewer rats and fleas, though this condition was certainly not due to any effort on the part of the proprietor. Fleas did well only if they had something to feed on. The proprietor had no dogs, and virtually no customers. Few people could stand to be around him, so it was tough on the fleas. Most of the fleas had probably starved to death.

The main event was a couple of tired, over-the-hill whores who plied their dismal trade on grubby unmade beds. The place also offered for rent, dismal, rat-hole rooms that smelled of sweat and urine. Like the owner, nothing had been scrubbed in years. The place was a dump.

Cheyenne found it by following the flies. When he arrived, the place did nothing to improve his mood. He walked in and glanced at the slob behind the bar. The man was a "no-neck" with huge hands, one continuous eyebrow, and the eyes of a cobra, which looked as though he hated everything.

Besides the grungy, slob-type barman, the place was peopled by a passed-out cowhand, and an aging hooker. The cowhand was sound asleep at a grubby round table, with one arm hanging straight down toward the floor. His other arm was slung across the table, holding fast to the other side like he was steering the saloon with a ship's wheel.

The grandma hooker started a tired and pathetic slink toward the new money. Cheyenne held up his hand and the woman stopped. The old bag knew trouble when she saw it.

Looking at the big slob behind the bar, Cheyenne hissed,

"I want some information. I'm looking for two men. Their names are Harnaky and Saunders."

The man behind the bar was mute in bluff. Cheyenne was sure he was a lousy poker player. In a flash, Cheyenne staked one of the big slob's huge hands to the wooden bar with his big knife, and then he proceeded to break the index finger on the guy's gun hand. The slob was talking before his first broken finger; he wasn't willing to risk a second. He shouted,

"They're in the back. They're in the back."

Then, realizing he was still pinned to the bar, he begged,

"Get me loose. Get me loose," The guy was in a lot of hurt.

"Who else is back there?"

"No one, just the guys and Mary Anne, one of the girls.

“Please, pull the knife,” he whispered through rotting, gritted teeth.

Williams ignored him, left him pinned where he was, and went hunting for the two men.

The area was a dark warren of rooms on one side of a hall very like a row of box stalls, but not good enough for horses. Cheyenne walked softly and listened. He saw a woman open a door, come out, and then run rapidly down the hall to a back exit. The child killing bastards knew he was there. He would have to smoke them out. He opened the first door, nothing, and then the second door and still nothing. Suddenly, two shots were fired right through the wall. They missed him, but not by much.

Now he knew where at least one of them was. Cheyenne could move like a ghost. Their klunky cow boots were nearly impossible to keep mouse quiet, but his Apache moccasins were perfect ghost shoes. And it was that simple. He simply waited. When a man came out to have a look, Cheyenne placed his hand over the man’s mouth, slit his throat and the man died silently. Cheyenne laid the dead man down soundlessly. Again he waited with Indian patience.

Cheyenne knew where his quarry was. The man was nervous. He couldn’t remain still, and when he moved he made noise, not much, but enough. When Cheyenne was sure where the man was within the room, he shot twice, a few inches apart, through the wall, and struck him dead center.

"You've killed me, I'm gut shot. Come and finish the job."

Williams didn't buy it, not yet. It could be a ruse. After listening to the man groan for many minutes, Cheyenne had a look. The man was on the floor. Cheyenne could see two red blood streaks where the fellow had slid down the wall and there was a pool of blood forming on the floor under him.

"Were you with the others in the raid on the Cheyenne Indian village?"

"It doesn't matter now."

"It does to me. Tell me the truth, otherwise I'll leave you here to die slowly."

"I didn't want to go along, but they paid us. My partner said we needed the money. At least I didn't kill any of the children."

"Who did?"

"Thorpe, he's an arrogant bastard. Calls himself Charles Thorpe. He's some kind of a nut. When he killed those Indians, he was laughing." The man's voice was suddenly cut off as he paused to wait out a spasm of wrenching pain.

"What's your name?"

"Name's Harnnaky, I didn't always ride with such a low crowd."

"Mr. Harnnaky, I'm not impressed."

Having said that, Williams shot him through the heart. Then he carved a large W on the man's chest. It was the well-known " Wims" brand of death. Cheyenne wanted the fellow's sleazy comrades to know whom to look for.

Cheyenne returned to the saloon to recover his knife. He found the slob bartender still staked to the bar by the big knife. Cheyenne pulled the knife from the hand and the bar. The man fainted. There were a zillion flies feasting on his hand, a few drinking from his slightly opened eyes, and the women were gone. The cowhand was still steering the saloon down some imaginary river, toward a place in his dreams that had to be better than the dump he was in at the moment. Cheyenne grabbed the drunk by the collar and dragged him to a safe distance outside. Then he returned and set fire to the building. He figured the heat would revive the slob long enough to forget about his hand and run for his life; if not, good riddance. He sat down, leaned against a tree, poured himself a drink of whisky and watched the place burn to the ground.

An hour later he sold a sack full of short guns, four rifles, some saddles and a string of horses to three greedy merchants in Warm Springs. Things were looking up and his mood was much improved. When Cheyenne Williams rode away, the cowhand was lying safely in the shade and still out cold.

CHAPTER FOUR

Cheyenne Williams felt tired clear through. He had ridden a hundred miles to his gold stash and sacked enough nuggets to last him for many months. The gold in his pockets cheered him more than somewhat. It never occurred to Cheyenne that he might be in debt to the gods, plural, when he traded gold nuggets for gold coins. He simply grinned like the proverbial Cheshire cat. He thought life was to be enjoyed, even in this harsh land, and when he wasn't fighting, he did enjoy life. But then, he often enjoyed fighting too, particularly so when he was leaning hard on nasty people. But for now he had had enough of that kind of man. There was just one more stop before he could have some down time.

As promised, he returned to the man who had owned the carved steer horn grip pistols, and found him dead. He had been severely mauled and partially eaten. The devastation and prints on the ground said grizzly bear. Ironically, the grizzly bear was a protective spirit of chief Kua Tonta and his people, and the chief had worn a necklace of grizzly bear claws all of his adult life.

Cheyenne grimaced slightly as he realized the macabre ending of the shooter. At rare times like this, he was more Indian than white, and almost a believer, almost, but not quite.

Williams was trashed of mind and body. It had been an arduous few weeks, and he was once again looking for a place to hang his hat. A few days later before arriving at the next town, he was trailing the shod horse hoof prints of the raiders and was looking carefully at the ground to examine the hoof prints, when he heard a rifle shot. A bullet missed his head by a gnat's eyelash as he jumped off his horse and dived for cover. His horse seemed to be unharmed and ran only a short distance before he stopped. The nag had been shot at before, but like his boss, he never quite got used to it.

Cheyenne thought this shooter must be a whacko. No one knew he was here. Just where he was, he didn't even know exactly. He wondered who the hell shot at strangers for no reason. So he asked the presumed whacko,

"Why the hell are you shooting at me? I'm new around here. I've only just arrived this minute so I can't be involved in any of your local problems."

A female voice shouted back,

"How can I be sure of that?"

"Well, I guess you can't, ma'm, but take a look at my horse. He's lathered some more than a local ride."

The voice said,

"Who are you?"

"My name is Cheyenne Williams, ma'm, and I'm just passing through."

"Are you that Cheyenne Williams?"

"As far as I know there is only one. It's a rough life. No one else would want it. People shoot at you for no reason."

"Oh, I had a reason. And I didn't miss. That bullet went where I wanted it to go.

"Then you must be one hell of a shot, lady."

"I am, Mr. Williams, I am. Now, I'm coming out. Stand real still until I get up close. I want to look you in the eye." And he did and she did.

When she got there, Williams was surprised to see how young and pretty she was. Her rather deep voice made her sound older than her apparent late teen look. Her first words up close were,

"God damn, you're good looking,"

She had Tennessee or Kentucky hills written all over her. She was a real down home rustic. She wore a huge beater hat that flopped every which-way, and home made bib overalls that looked as though there was nothing under them but ripe woman. On each side she was naked from shoulder to hips. She had on funny farmers shoes and carried a well cared for Kentucky long-rifle.

Her hair was very thick and white blonde. Her very bright, light blue eyes were smiling and she wore a mega-watt smile that would stop trains. Her peek-a-boo overalls showed she had a body equal to, if not better than, the Goddess Diana.

Cheyenne was ready to forgive her for shooting at him. He thought meeting this gorgeous kitten surely beat the hell out of an otherwise boring ride.

Her next words were,

"I bet I can shoot as good as you!"

"It's well, and I'll bet you can't."

He didn't want any more proof of her shooting skill.

"What's going on around here that would cause you to shoot that close to a stranger?"

"Did you see movement back yonder on the hillside to the right of the trail?"

Cheyenne admitted he did see something out of the corner of his eye, but couldn't be certain because of the dense cover.

"That was me. That horse of yours can sure cover ground. I've been running through the woods to keep up. When I thought you might get away, I decided to fire that shot."

Smiling big as life, she said,

"And it worked, didn't it, cause here you are."

"You looked so fancy, I just didn't want you to get away. I wanted you to go swimming with me. It's so damn hot and the stream is not far."

"Girl, a simple introduction would have sufficed."

"You talk funny."

"Girl. What the hell are you doing out here in Wyoming in the first place?"

"I've been waiting for you."

"How old are you?"

"Eighteen and full grown, so what's it going to be? Yes, or no, cause it's too hot to stand here and argue!"

Cheyenne didn't think he was looking at "supplies," {his word for getting laid} but he thought the stream did sound like a great idea.

"Miss, I'll have to admit you've got my attention," he said, taking his foot out of the stirrup. The girl said,

"No, not that way. Come on over here to this stump."

She ran to a tall stump and waited until he was along side, and then leaped onto the saddle in front of him, still carrying her rifle. Gripping the horse with her legs, she lowered her lush derriere slowly down onto his lap so as not to give him a high voice. Then she turned her head and gave him her train-stopping smile. Cheyenne was already bewitched. He would have championed her cause just to see her smile.

He smiled and merely said,

"Where to?"

She pointed and said again,

"God damn, you're good looking."

They arrived at the stream after a ten-minute ride. He was sure the girl could feel his enlarging cock because every now and then she wiggled her beautiful little derriere against it. She didn't say a word the entire ride. He pushed her forward, stood up in the stirrups, made some adjustments and carefully sat back down again. It was to be a disconcerting ride for each of them.

//////

Cheyenne saw the stream was beautifully clear and perhaps five feet deep in the pools. It meandered this way and that through thick green tree areas and some open meadow. When she told him to stop, he could see a small sandy beach just below a lush grassy area near the trees. The place had it all. Hot sun, lush grass in both the sun and the shade, and beautifully shaded bowers beneath some very large, old cottonwood and willow trees.

The girl tossed her leg over the neck of his horse, slid to the ground, walked to the stream and sat down on the bank. Cheyenne thought he saw a glazed look in her eye.

Cheyenne dismounted like people and tried to look as if he didn't have an erection as he tied his horse in the shade. He noticed the girl already had her shoes off and was working on her bib over-alls. If it were to be a race, she would win because he was wearing more than four pieces of clothing.

She stood up and her bib over-alls accordioned down around her ankles. Then she stepped out of them with the grace of a ballerina. Last, she tossed her big floppy hat on the ground and was immediately transformed into a lesser Goddess. Cheyenne, who thought he had seen everything where women were concerned, was marginally stunned.

When the girl finished undressing, she waited for him as though they had both done this every day of their lives. She didn't look at him, which gave him a little time to get his dick back to nearly normal. When he was finished undressing, he dived into the water and the cool water did the rest. He swam near where she was on the bank, and stopped when he was still hip deep.

She again remarked how handsome he was. Women had been telling him this all of his life and he paid little attention, but for reasons that weren't clear to him, when this girl said it, he liked to hear it.

"I'm glad you think so."

Candidly, she said,

"Please don't go into the water just yet. Come on out for a few minutes. I want to look at you for a little while."

"It was necessary, as you are very well aware, young lady. I'm not used to having such a beautiful little ass bouncing against me while on horseback."

She confided,

"You know, I was having the strangest feelings, too. I could feel you back there and I liked it. It made me feel kinda warm down there."

He got out of the water and walked up close to her.

She noticed he was wearing two knives on a belt around his waist. She said,

"What are those for?"

He didn't answer her but suggested that she carry a knife and keep her rifle close to the shore when she went swimming.

"This is sometimes not nice country. One cannot be too careful."

Suddenly changing moods, he said,

"Now young lady, I want to look at you as well. You really are a great visual feast."

He mused to himself that without her clothes, the girl was absolutely stunning in every way.

"Wow, no one ever said that to me before. That's one of the reasons I stopped you. I don't know any other young women, so I have nothing to compare me with. I was hoping you could tell me some things."

He could see she was genuinely concerned about herself stacking up against other women. He assumed there must be a young man in her life.

She continued with her examination and asked him to slowly turn around for her. She said it as if she expected him to do it.

He said,

"I will, but only if you will do the same for me."

He did and she said,

"Mr. Williams, you are the most beautiful man I have ever seen."

"Thank you, ma'm," he said, smiling and bowing slightly. For reasons that weren't clear, he did not feel ridiculous. Perhaps it was her fresh innocence.

"Girl, now it's your turn. Hold your arms out a little and slowly turn around."

"Not so fast. Turn slower,"

"That's better."

She did and she liked it, and she said so. She continued further with the comment,

"I can see in your eyes that you like looking at me, too, and I am glad, so very glad."

"Girl, most men would like to look at you this way. You really are stunningly beautiful, and I mean that."

The girl beamed.

She had a perfect physical structure. Cheyenne had never seen better. Her body, which was small boned and darkly tanned all over, was wonderfully contrasted with her wild mop of long, thick, white-blond hair that hung half way down her back. In front her beautiful hair hung down far enough to partially, yet provocatively cover each breast. She had a small elegant head on a beautiful neck that flowed into strong shoulders. The girl possessed a very beautiful oval face with very intense, light blue eyes. She had a small, straight nose over a rather large mouth with generous lips. She even had a pleasant, deep sounding voice. The girl was wondrously adorned with rather ample, high round breasts, a tiny waist, and beautiful hips followed by gorgeous, lovely, long, strong legs. She had a derriere that women would kill for and men would roll their eyes skyward in a variety of lusty prayers. Her pubic hair was only a little darker than the white-blonde fluff on her head. And lastly, she was gifted with elegant hands and feet. The girl was one of God's own best sculptures.

Eyeing this treasure, thinking she was one fancy lady, Cheyenne decided that he had better tell her his thoughts. And later, he did. Fortunately for him, it took much longer than he expected.

Interrupting his thought pattern, the girl said,

"Let's swim now. We can talk later."

They waded in from the sandy beach. The stream was crystal clear and cool enough to be refreshing. She spent a lot of time swimming underwater, swimming close to him, then swimming away, then back again, all without touching. Her hair pulled by the current, was like a great cloud at times and then smoothed out like seal fur as she stroked underwater. He followed her pattern; except when she attempted to swim away he stayed close to her. They swam through sunlight and shadow patches in the stream, and even saw a few fish Cheyenne, looking at this kitten, was smiling clear through. When they both went up for air, he gave a deep laugh and she looked curiously at him. He said, standing on the bottom of the stream,

"Girl, you make me feel good."

"You make me feel strange," she said simply.

"I think I want you to kiss me." And she glided over to him without waiting for his consent, stood up, and kissed him. The girl was tall and willowy and she melted into him like his second skin. He was astonished by how good she felt to his touch. This girl was unbelievable. He had held few women in his life that had felt that great in his arms. There was something naïve, and at the same time, very purposeful and womanly sensual about her.

Her kiss told of a hunger that wouldn't stop with just one kiss. She pushed her breasts against him and kissed him again. After the kiss, she held on to him very tightly for several moments, and he held on to her. It was an affectionate moment that was new and different for them both. She took his hand and led him out of the water.

This girl certainly had his attention. He said,

"I would never have thought getting shot at could be so pleasant. You certainly do have a different approach."

They both smiled at the tangential humor.

"You were safe. I told you I always hit what I aim at, except in your case, I missed what I intended to miss."

Moments later she looked seriously at him and asked,

"Do you know anything about women?"

He smiled and thought to himself, does the sun rise in the east? But answered,

"A little."

"I want you to make love to me. I want you to teach me every thing you think I should know about making love. Show me and explain things."

"Miss, are you a virgin?"

"Yes," she answered simply.

"I've been watching the road for three months, hoping the right person would come along to teach me. You're the right person. I can tell by the way you kiss me."

He liked her candor, but was beginning to feel like a specimen.

"Miss, virgins are not my style. I prefer a more serious romper than any virgin is likely to be. Besides, there must be some young men around here."

There is one, but he's a virgin, too, because he's caught up in all that religious stuff. We kissed one time and there was nothing in it for either of us. That's what got me to thinking maybe I need to know more than to just rely on Mother Nature. Paw said when I meet the right man I'd know what to do and Mother Nature would do the rest.

We have a horse ranch and I've seen how the mares behave with the stallions. Paw says they get "horny."

"Mr. Williams, I want you to get me horny,"

"Girl, are you sure you know what you are doing? This is not like changing hats, you know. You will be changed forever. Not all women look forward to the experience, but afterward, most are glad they had it."

Cheyenne laughed at the situation. A young goddess was practically begging him to seduce her, and he was half-heartedly attempting, to talk her out of it. She discussed her virginity as though she were trading horses. She may not be very sophisticated about men and knew nothing of them in a sexual way, but her smarts department worked well enough.

Apparently, the discussion was concluded in her mind because she slithered up beside Cheyenne for another kiss, and got one, a nice long one.

"Oh, my. That was nice. Do it again."

They kissed many times. Her lips were insistent, soft, and hungry. By then, so were his. He interrupted her, went to his horse, shook out his bedroll, and placed it on the ground and then went back to the girl.

She waited with glazed eyes. He walked to her and kissed her hair and her neck. He kissed her mouth and probed with his tongue, while she pushed her pubic area against his rising manhood. Then he kissed her breasts and her eyes rolled back. Cheyenne put her hand on his erection.

"Ohhhh."

Next he moved her hand back and forth and then she put both hands on it.

"Ohhh, Wow, Wow!"

Once more being candid, she asked,

"Can a woman really take all of that?"

"Yes, if they want to."

"I want to, I want to. Oh, it's so beautiful. You make me so excited. I'm so excited I can't stand it. I guess I'm "horny" now, because I want you. I want you now."

Without letting go, she led him by his dick to the bedroll and sat down. The girl leaned back and spread her legs. Cheyenne, now beside her, ran his hands over her breasts, and then slowly moved his hands down to her pubic area. He gently probed and stroked inside as she eagerly raised her hips to meet his hand.

Cheyenne was pleased to find her more than ready for him before she sat down, and now she was lost in a pleasure zone of her own. He discovered the girl could say a lot with a single word as she continued with,

"Ohhh!"

"Ohhh!"

And finally,

"That's so good!

At the point of mounting her he stroked her with the end of his manhood, back and forth across the entry a few times. She pushed up to receive him and he explained,

"This may hurt for a brief moment. I'm going to move in very slowly."

"Oh, oh, ooooh!"

She had her hands on his hips. When he stopped, she pulled him farther into her. He moved in very slowly till he felt bottom. When he backed out, she whispered,

"No, no. Please don't go away, it's soooo goood," and she pulled him into her again. He was in nearly all the way, but not moving. He waited a long moment and then began to move in and out, in and out. She loved it. The girl rolled her head one way and then the other saying,

"It's sooo good. It's sooo good. Oh, wow. It's sooo good!"

She was on cloud nine. In a minute she screamed, climaxed with a gut wrenching orgasm, the kind where the girl bucks several times before settling down to gasp for breath, and finally to purr.

She went through that sequence many times before they rested.

Cheyenne, the pro, knew a fireball when he found one. Still inside her and with only a few small scratches, he laid still, kissing her hair. When he looked at her watching him, he saw tears in her eyes.

"I am so happy, so happy. Thank you, Thank you." Then she squeezed him and squealed,

"Eeeeeooooow. I never dreamed anything could be so beautiful, so wonderful. Can we do it again?"

"Girl, we are just getting started. When this day is over, you'll know every position and everything you own will be sore, even your hair will hurt, but it will have been worth it."

"Show me, show me now."

And he most certainly did.

//////

Two hours later they were both satiated and lying on his bedroll, when she once again said, "Wow!"

Cheyenne was mute. He was thinking, "This girl is fabulous and I nearly passed her by. For every move I made, she made one of her own, even some I've never seen before. It's difficult to believe she was a virgin. She certainly is a natural. She's already more woman than most of the women I've known. She is certainly the most enthusiastic pupil I've ever had."

He thought back to the great days of Miss Moresby, and his own days as an enthusiastic pupil. We all learn from someone, but it's best to learn from experts. He was glad that she had "honored" him. She had also taught him something about human nature. Life was indeed, full of surprises. She helped to reinforce the idea that being single, for him, was really the only way to go. He was pleased with himself, at the moment. And he was very well pleased with her.

She broke into his reverie with the question,

"Penny for your thoughts?"

"They're worth more. I was evaluating you in my mind and being very grateful to you. Girl, you have really honored me. You are very special. You are a whole lot better than most women. We both found out what you wanted to know, and I am thankful that you chose to share yourself with me."

"I am pleased to hear you say that. I did so want to please you and I'm glad that I have. You have made me very happy," she stated sincerely.

They were both silent for a long moment.

"Is there anything more that you could teach me?"

"Yes, but it might be best if you waited for awhile."

"Why, I'm all woman. You said so yourself and damn it, I want to know."

"Aren't you a little sore?"

"Sore, Hell, yes, I'm sore; I can hardly walk, for Chrisake. But like you said, it was certainly worth it and I still want to learn all I can. I want to learn it all; I want to learn everything you ever heard of before you go. You are liable to be gone the minute I turn my back, and I won't even have a chance to practice some of the things you've taught me."

"O.K. Girl. I won't go anywhere until you have experienced most of it."

The girl beamed. She even clapped her hands, the only part of her that didn't hurt.

"Most of it? What do you mean, most of it? I want to learn it all."

"There are some things I don't do."

Her curiosity aroused, she jumped on his statement.

"What things?"

"Never mind."

//////

After a little whiskey and a while later, he said,

"Girl, the lesson starts now. Lie down!"

She was surprised, gave him a look of mild concern, her big train-stopping smile, a look of serious interest and her undivided attention.

Then her eyes got big as saucers and finally they rolled back until only the whites showed.

CHAPTER FIVE

With a promise to the girl to return when his work was finished, Cheyenne reluctantly rode away. Three weeks later, with another raider under, Williams was tired of the vengeance trail. He was camped with the coyotes on the way to nowhere.

He knew getting laid was better than knocking heads, anytime. What he didn't understand was why some men didn't seem to know the difference. Usually it was the power guys: generals, politicians, big business types, bankers, railroad builders and the like. He wondered why they were confused over the issue.

Cheyenne had said on several occasions that Custer would have been better off to remain in that whorehouse forever rather than to seek glory at the Little Big Horn. Cheyenne had said as much to the general, just a few days before the man rode out to the battlefield to meet the Sioux. Cheyenne followed his own shrewd advice, and stayed put. He refused to fight the Sioux, as he had many friends among the Lakota, and at the time he wasn't broke.

Cheyenne reasoned that any man, who left a whorehouse while he still had money in his pocket, was either two hundred years old, or his smart box was "around the bend." He knew for a fact that one or two of those "doves" could suck the works right out of the average vest-pocket watch. With that thought looming large in his mind, he stood drunkenly, raised his glass, and said something in a dialect from a far off Indian tribe, laughed, and drank a silent toast to such singular skill.

When the report of the Battle of the Little Bighorn came back, Cheyenne Williams drank another toast to both sides. He realized the one redeeming feature of the entire event was that he would not have to listen to any more ridiculous discourse about the proper care of the gonads from a health-nut general.

He was weary. He was looking at the stars and thinking of the girl. He would continue his search, but he missed the girl more than he cared to admit.

//////

Several days later, Williams was still riding the vengeance trail. He was as cranky as an old bear. He had lost weight and so had his horse. They were both worn down from long rides without much to show for it. They both needed a rest. The others could wait. He, at last, knew where most of the village raiders were.

At the time, he just wanted a meal and a bath and to sleep the clock around. Then he would find some "supplies." He liked society's euphemisms and had added a couple of his own. "Supplies" was one of them. "Replacement stock" was another.

Women were an area of human endeavor he considered a high art form. He usually embraced life with exceptional enthusiasm; the fun stuff, like women, even more so. But first, he needed a place to rest, and to get cleaned up.

//////

He came to a thriving cow town that had been only a wide spot on the prairie when he was last there. The place had a good bar, a dance hall, and a fairly decent hotel with edible food. The hotel even stocked a few good wines.

Cheyenne decided that this burg would do just fine. During his manhunt he had taken out a few more heinous killers. He had spent some of his outrage and was tired of killing.

He stabled his horse with the usual warnings about the critter to the livery help; then he went next door to the blacksmith to order new horseshoes. He made an appointment with the farrier because he had to be there to keep his bronc from wrecking the guy's shop. He bought ammo, whiskey, some new clothes, and moved into the Hotel Victoria.

His arrival triggered a bustle of activity and excitement among the otherwise rather bored, female staff members. The word was already out about the arrival of an extremely attractive new guest.

The hotel proprietor was an obvious admirer of most things English. Those same things, Williams regarded with singular disdain, and the proprietor with contempt. He chose to ignore his natural call for mischief, because the pompous ass did own the only decent hotel for hundreds of miles and the fellow employed a number of attractive women.

As he entered his room there were maids, a woman clerk, a waitress and several female guests passing by his room like ants around a picnic. Further scouting gave rise to new intelligence. The several smiles and admiring glances he received suggested that he was, indeed, a fox in a hen house. He wondered if the hotel owner considered the ladies his own private stock, or did he merely have an avuncular role?

Standing in the buff, fairly rippling with muscles and old battle-scars, Williams had a whiskey bottle in one hand, a glass in the other, and still wearing his hat, admired himself in the large, full-length mirror. He was pleased with what he saw. The women who had seen him this way were also pleased with what they had seen and for a variety of reasons. In fact, most of them were ecstatic. His moment of reverie was interrupted when the hotel boy came in carrying two large buckets of hot water for Cheyenne's bath.

The boy was assisted shortly afterward, by a coterie of three lithe, young and lovely, nubile, giggling volunteers, all of whom were rewarded with a very up-close look at our hero.

Hoping to get a peek at the much talked about new guest, they calmly walked in carrying buckets of hot water, only to be confronted by the magnificent figure of Cheyenne Williams standing buck-naked and ankle deep in a huge copper bathtub. They squealed with delight and confusion, put down the buckets, put their hands to their mouths, gaped, and stood as if frozen to the floor. It was no wonder. Williams was indeed, a magnificent physical specimen. Cheyenne laughed, a deep rumbling laughter, that was heard all of the way down the hall to the lobby.

The girls, a moment later and no longer spellbound in their nervous excitement, literally ran in circles and then into each other. Cheyenne smiling, tipped his hat, bowed slightly to them and with his left hand still holding the whiskey bottle, gestured toward the open door, and said politely,

"Ladies."

They regained their composure, giggled, and left reluctantly, each with several backward glances as they withdrew. Cheyenne had made their day, their week and perhaps even their year. It might be a tough act for their young men to follow, but at least the girls had an idea of what physical attributes they might look for in the future.

Williams, laughing, still wearing his hat standing in the tub, poured himself a drink, and proposed a toast to the girls' future womanly maturity. He said aloud to no one in particular,

"To replacement stock." And he drank down a couple of fingers of rather good scotch.

Some time later, scrubbed and clean, Cheyenne was deeply submerged in the huge copper tub with his booze at hand. He was still amused by the behavior of the young ladies and thoroughly enjoying himself. He thought that if he had known about the hotel and it's occupants, he would have come here sooner.

Lithe, young stuff, in general, was not his style, but they had provided him with his biggest laugh in a long, long time. The three nubile nymphs in the bucket brigade needed a couple of years to round out, in order to catch his eye. He much preferred women who were more ripe and rounded. He called them "Rubenesque."

In his recent memory, there was a well-remembered young nubile with flaxen hair, when he had made an exception, much to his delight, but she was an exception to the rule. His rule called for ripe, curvaceous women, twenty five to thirty five years of age, experienced with a slightly naughty, no holds barred attitude. The rule was very elastic, and only worked if he was surrounded by "supplies." During lean times on the trail he was inclined to go a little older or younger in age and give some slack toward attitude.

///////

Cheyenne began to think of the Hotel Victoria as possibly a major source of "supplies." A few moments later, he was sure of it.

Just as he got out of the tub, a young attractive woman slipped through the door to his room and locked it from the inside. She carried a jacket, was wearing a nearly see-through blouse, a long wrap-around skirt, riding boots, and nothing else. In her eyes there was a serious look of lust. She stripped in seconds. Without taking her eyes off Cheyenne, she walked over to him, put her hands on his chest and slowly rubbed him up and down. Then, putting her arms around his neck, she kissed him and he kissed back. Cheyenne had great fun with all of this. It seemed the Hotel Victoria was full of surprises, the rare and good kind.

"Why the indecision?" he said smiling.

She ignored the light sarcasm as if she didn't want to lose her concentration. Giving him her first coy look, she dropped her last garment, a pretty, burgundy colored ribbon-garter and she announced,

"Now we have matching costumes"

"Not quite, he said, I'm still wearing my hat. Your costume is perfect, but where's your hat?"

"I saw you on the street when you arrived and I just had to come."

"You will."

"I told them at the desk, I was your sister. What do you say to a little incest?"

"Miss, do I know you?"

"No, but we're working on it," and she began to towel him off.

"Wow, would you look at that!"

She never got to his feet.

Two hours later she was smiling and worn out.

"I believe I have been ravaged and I know I was impaled," she offered seriously.

He was wearing a big dumb satisfied grin. They were both sitting up in bed sipping straight whiskey. He'd offered her some while saying,

"Here, this will revive you for the next round."

She looked astonished; her mouth opened, but remained mute.

The girl was really good and Cheyenne, knowing major skill when he found it, was not about to let her get away.

He kissed her hair affectionately and sat back smiling. The girl melted, gave a big sigh, put on a pleased look, held out her hand and said,

"By the way, my name is Dallas Manning. And if you say the obvious, I'll hit you."

Cheyenne grinned some more and reached over to shake her hand, saying,

"Well, Dallas Manning, my name is Cheyenne Williams. She took his hand, kissed it, and placed it on her left breast. The woman was very well built. Her breasts were high and round and very well filled Cheyenne's big hands. He looked at her and said,

"Merry Christmas, beautiful. You really are beautiful, all over."

"So are you, handsome man, so are you," she purred, as she slid down his frame for more.

CHAPTER SIX

Later, in the dining room, both of them were all dressed up, and Cheyenne and Dallas were still wearing a glow from making love. People were surprised to see Williams with a female guest so soon. The word "sister" cruised around the dining room on the tongues of the gossips, spoken by the forward ladies, and whispered by the shy timid ones. Some women, the seriously envious, said it with obvious doubt. The green with envy, and the all-purpose vicious women, were convinced Dallas Manning was "the bitch from Hell."

The Hotel Victoria had indeed, proven to be a "source of supplies." One might even say, "a supply house."

Though he rarely made this big a stir in the world of men unless he was fighting, he was accustomed to getting the attention of women easily enough. He wasn't always successful in his pursuits, but he was pragmatic enough to live by the axiom, "if he shook enough trees, he would get apples."

He thought to himself, metaphorically, his dinner guest was a whole bushel of very ripe apples. He told her he was plying her with nourishment to build up her strength. She gave him a charming and challenging smile, and he could tell that this apple had staying power. Cheyenne could not have been more pleased. He had, indeed, found "supplies," and with great legs.

In Cheyenne's day a lady dressed so as to be covered from head to toe. Poets would frequently write of the exotic excitement aroused just from seeing the milk white skin of a lady's wrist. Fashionable gloves were deliberately made with several buttonholes that when buttoned showed a series of small elliptical windows. The lady glove wearers were convinced these "erogenous views" of their wrists were very risqué. To Cheyenne's way of thinking the concept was so subtle, it was ludicrous and non-existent. His idea of a turn-on was a sensuously hungry beauty that wanted to tear him in half, a woman who couldn't wait to fuck his brains out, and he'd certainly found one. This provocative fireball was at that moment dining across from him in a cozy booth, and having removed her shoe, was pawing his inner thigh and his groin with her bare foot. He was convinced she had prehensile toes. This was a fun surprise. He shared her enthusiasm for her various skills.

She delicately put the end of a small baby back rib into her mouth, licked her fingers, and at the same time, made pleasantly naughty and suggestive moves with her tongue and lips. Cheyenne laughed appreciatively. This girl had style.

Cheyenne Williams had known many a serious and well-remembered romper, but very few who were seemingly effortlessly provocative all the time. He began to wonder if she might be a keeper. She certainly had his attention. He began to look beyond her superbly, well rounded form. He looked at the little things, the corners of her well shaped mouth, the thickness of her cushion lips, the pretty little curls of hair on the back of her neck. He liked her hair, particularly the little ones at the base of her head that transitioned into the beautiful, dark, thick mass. The gorgeous stuff was usually piled high on her head and held precariously in place by a large comb. When down, her hair would hang low enough to partially and seductively cover her magnificent breasts. The girl was indeed a major visual statement and she was getting to him.

Cheyenne was very likely the last pushover in the world where women were concerned. He usually regarded them much like horses; they were necessary and useful tools. Some women were just a little more skilled than others. One time, riding the trail, he mused if he had to make a choice between women and horses, it would probably depend on just how far he had to walk. One did not take women seriously. He euphemistically referred to them for years as "supplies," and ironically, at the same time, he regarded them with reverence.

Over the years, he had helped, rescued and saved, any number of female types, including little children and old people from all sorts of horribles; not so where men were concerned. His attitude toward men was "to Hell with them." Let them take care of themselves. If they couldn't "hack it," then they shouldn't be out there. The West was no place for lightweights. He thought the West had far too many men in it any way, a large portion of whom, were scoundrels.

Cheyenne, in fact, had helped a few men over the years: several Indian chiefs of different tribes, in a number of different battles, and he had helped Zero Smith in the Pinedale War.

//////

Cheyenne Williams had not lost sight of the fact that he was riding a vengeance trail. He was still after the killers of the people in the Cheyenne village. He had merely taken a much-needed rest.

After meeting the insatiable Dallas Manning, the rest was very likely to be extended indefinitely. The bad guys would still be there. Cheyenne Williams was one western rascal who had his priorities straight.

//////

Cheyenne certainly enjoyed life at the Hotel Victoria. Dallas continued to be her provocative self as she waded through her meal with seductive pleasure. After they finished, and were returning to their room, they discovered to their delight, a rare event, a string quartet in the lobby. The insatiate pair took chairs expectantly, rubbed knees, and listened. The music was beautiful. Dallas made it through Mozart and Brahms to the intermission. Then she stood up and whispered to Cheyenne, loud enough for all to hear,

"God damn it, that's enough. You are going to be my next composer."

With that she plowed through the audience with Cheyenne in tow, and charged the stairway to their room with all the determination of Hannibal crossing the Alps. Tongues wagged as the two prime specimens departed. Many women in the room were green with envy. Two or three severely "bored marrieds," were ready to kill themselves.

The next morning at breakfast, Dallas was purring. The sharp edges had disappeared and in their place she wore a solid, satisfied look of contentment. She even glowed. Cheyenne, seated across from her, wore a big dumb grin of his own, the good kind. The girl hadn't crippled him, but she was working on it. A few more days of this lusty behavior and he would have to hit the trail to rest up.

Our hero found himself with an enviable decision regarding the lady Dallas, more, or lots more? He decided a few more days of Dallas was essential to his well being and continued good spirits. Rapport with his "Mistai," good spirits" was a major consideration because they came from several cultures: Indian, African, Hawaiian, white, and of course, liquid. His recently discovered "glory hole" in the cottonwood tree root, also made a major contribution to his general well being and to his peace of mind.

He wondered if he should tell her just what he was doing in this part of the country. Likewise, what was she doing here? The subject had never come up. He realized he knew nothing about her. What was to know? She was smart as a whip, had a wonderful sense of humor, looked great, and fucked like a mink! He could live with that, and was grateful for it.

The very next day Dallas made it easy for him when she said,

"I must be getting back to my people. I've been away too long.

If you want to find me, leave a note at the desk. I'll arrange to have it picked up." She didn't offer to explain and he didn't ask.

Within the hour, they were both out of the hotel. They said "goodbye" and left in different directions. It was rather anticlimactic and he missed her immediately.

CHAPTER SEVEN

Cheyenne Williams had made a few inquiries when in town, and learned for a price from the stable man, that two of the men he sought, were believed to have been recently hired at the big spread northeast of town. The ranch started just outside of town and the main cow camp was about twenty miles away. On the ride, Cheyenne could see the ranch was a paradise for cattle and horses and because of the great distances, likely to be rough on men. There was grass as far as the eye could see, meadowlands with wild flowers, and many small creeks from the higher up snowmelt. There were areas of grass close to very thick timber where a smart cow, if she were lucky, could hide well into her old age. There was also plenty of brush and loose rock.

Every ranch had a few old cows with splayed feet which were all horn, hide and bones, and showed up at gather time. The perturbed rancher would scratch his head and wonder where the hell the old girls had been all of those years?

In his mind, Cheyenne could hear the often asked, old questions, and he smiled at the thought.

"In the brush, old Hoss, that's where."

"Yeah, but how could we have missed these old girls, year after year, for so long."

"Easily."

He could see the Indians smiling too. They didn't have that problem with the buffalo.

Cheyenne had been seeing cattle for sometime. Most of them were wearing a slash dash seven brand / -7. The big brand was placed on the right side of the cows. A small slash dash seven was put high on the left hip of the horses. Cheyenne could read the signs as well as the brands. He was getting close to the big ranch headquarters.

Since he was part Indian, he didn't expect to be greeted with open arms, and he wasn't. He asked around for the foreman, and finally located a white haired, all-purpose, senior redneck. Cheyenne figured the guy was a bit "long in the tooth" to ramrod a ranch of this size, but one never knew. Maybe he was family. Williams wasn't given the common courtesy. He wasn't asked to step down.

When Cheyenne told him he was looking for two renegade, rapist-murderers, the man lost it.

"Ride on, mister. There's no one like that on this ranch. Now git."

When he saw Cheyenne wasn't turning his horse, he said,

"I can put twenty guns on you in two minutes."

"They won't help you. You'll be dead. Just listen to me, and then I'll leave. I have their names from a man who rode with them on the raid: Jennings and Malloy. Jennings has a walleye, and Malloy thinks he's a shooter. He wears a lot of black, black hat, black scarf, black cuffs and a black heart."

The foreman's eyes opened slightly wider.

"Then you've seen them. Perhaps hired them in the last few weeks?"

The man was non-committal. Foremen were usually a tight- lipped breed. After a long pause he asked,

"You the law?"

"No. Didn't know there was any around here."

"There isn't. But we keep hearing rumors that there might be soon."

"They killed some friends of mine. They even raped and killed some of the women and children."

"Women and children, you say?"

Cheyenne, a near atheist added for emphasis,

"God's truth."

"They rode in looking for work a few weeks back. I put them in a line cabin to do some small repair jobs. Far as I know, they are still up there."

"Follow that creek," he said, pointing, "and you'll come to the cabin. If I was you, I'd go fox careful."

"Much obliged."

As he turned his horse, Cheyenne added, "You'd better start looking for their replacements."

CHAPTER EIGHT

Cheyenne rode out at a canter and the big horse covered ground as though he loved to run. The big stud horse could canter through the better part of a day. Cheyenne's innards were looking for a hammock long before the big horse tired.

He found the pair of scoundrels hunkered down in the shade of the east wall of the cabin. He tied his horse and Injuned up to listen to Malloy, the shooter, grousing about the boredom.

"I'm getting real tired of this. It's hot. We're in the middle of nowhere. There's no women, no liquor, and you are a rotten cook. I think that about covers it, so let's ride. We can swing by and get our pay."

"Maybe you're right. After the raid we both agreed to lie low for a while, to let things settle down. It's been about five weeks. Maybe that's long enough."

"Hell, nobody cares about a few Indians anyway. Still, we shouldn't have done it. Killing kids is not our kind of work. Besides, the money was lousy."

"For Chrisake, man, we were dead broke and hungry, and like you say, nobody cares about a few dead Indians."

Cheyenne stepped around the corner and braced them.

"Wrong! I care about a few Indians! Make your play, boys."

The two men started to rise, went for their irons, and slid back down the wall, dead. Cheyenne had thrown two knives at the same time, into their throats. One man's spine was severed. As he fell over in death, his head tilted comically.

Jennings and Malloy would have eternity to contemplate the raid. Cheyenne had a good feeling about having put their lights out. They were vermin. He retrieved his knives and then, to clean up the camp for the next crew, he threw a heeler's catch around the feet of the two dead men and dragged their bodies a half mile into the pines and dropped the ropes. The gathering vultures would do the rest.

Cheyenne rode back to the cabin, gathered up the rest of the men's weapons and their horses, and headed northeast. He had acquired so much hardware his packhorse was beginning to rattle and the horses strung out behind him looked like a pack train. The list of crossed-off names was getting longer, and the list of names-to-do was getting shorter. He was nearly finished.

//////

Two days later, Cheyenne arrived at a grubby cow town. It was the sorriest place he'd seen in a long time. Nothing was painted. Nothing was square or quite in place. The street was badly rutted, fence posts were slanted, roofs sagged, porches were cock-eyed and of the few visible windows, it seemed that over half were broken and stuffed with rags. The town seemed to have an abundance of rags. No folks, just rags. Most towns reflected the people who lived there. This town seemed to state its persona by the ubiquitous rags.

So far, Cheyenne had not seen much activity.

It did have water. The village was a wide spot near a small stream. The stream came right out of the rock from a large spring. It had enough water volume to create a rippling sound as the water passed over the narrow, rocky streambed. Apparently, its sole purpose was to give life to the village, because shortly beyond the edge of town the stream just disappeared into the prairie grass.

Williams had seen entire rivers just disappear into the ground. Further north in the territory there was a river that divided into the Big Lost River and The Little Lost River, both of which flowed for a way and then just disappeared into the ground.

Williams found the next two men he was looking for, talking in a dark box stall in the back end of the town's only livery stable. They both wore big batwing chaps and large Mexican rowel spurs. He roped their heads together and conked their brainpans with his pistol. He then tossed the rope over a rafter, hooked his foot under a stall gate for leverage, and hanged them, in seconds. Only a very strong man could have done such a thing, but Cheyenne Williams was strong, very strong. As they swung, he carved a W on each man's chest. It was all done as quiet as a mouse.

He then went around to the front of the livery stable, found the owner, and sold him several horses, including those, which belonged to Jennings and Malloy. Next, he went to the general store and sold the proprietor a sack full of short guns and five rifles. He kept two rather good pistols for reasons that weren't clear to anyone, including himself.

CHAPTER NINE

After hanging the two rejects from Hell, Cheyenne went to what passed for a saloon. That's where all of the action was, both of them.

He was greeted with a big yawn behind the bar from the diminutive bartender, who apparently did not appreciate the interruption of his siesta. The scrawny, wizened, dried up, little man looked as though his next sleep would be his last. As if that weren't enough, the guy had help. There was another old geezer sound asleep on a bench in the corner. Like the first one, he too, looked as though death would be a blessing.

To get their attention, Cheyenne fired two shots, one through the roof and the other into a large spittoon. The big brass beast, bounced across the floor, spreading most of its reservoir of acquired "horribles." The place was so bad that Cheyenne doubted if any one would even notice. His big cannon woke up the two old guys, the local hooker upstairs, and what passed for a large part of the citizenry of the entire town. Three or four of the locals came on the run. They were sure the two old guys, who argued all of the time, had finally got fed up, and put each other's lights out.

They found the old boys were still alive and seemed disappointed. Then they started to give the old boys hell for the shooting, and for the interruption of the their customary siesta, until they saw Cheyenne.

Cheyenne had been in this no-place burg about six minutes, and he was already disgusted with it. He often wondered why people tried to squeeze out an existence in the most unlikely places. This was certainly one of them. Maybe the locals squeezed, but it didn't show. He was sure the locals and the town were losing the "them or us," battle for a meager existence, but they just didn't know it yet; probably never would. It appeared to Cheyenne that both the town and the people were in a slow, inevitable, spiral toward their own destruction. One day, when all of the young people were gone and the old folks had all died off, the sun and wind would reclaim the place. Over time, even the ghosts would move on for lack of interest, and the grass would return and slowly cover everything. The grass always won out in the end.

Cheyenne wondered if two shots brought half the town on the run, what their reaction would be when one of them discovered two hanged men swinging from the rafters in their livery stable.

The scrawny yawn got to his feet, first one and then the other, took a bearing, and crab-like, by hanging on to this and grabbing at that, crawled his way at near glacial speed toward Cheyenne. When the old man arrived, Cheyenne, waiting, considered it to be a singular achievement. He was ready to applaud the old boy who questioned,

"Something I can do for you?"

"Not likely, But I can do something for you."

"Yeah, And what's that?"

"I can let you live through the day."

From thirty feet away, Cheyenne threw his big knife and stuck it in the throat of a huge stuffed elk head that was mounted above the bar. The ancient's eyes got big and he started to get the shakes. Cheyenne thought to himself that none of these old guys had a very firm grip on life. He didn't realize that his own outrageous behavior was a primary cause of their fear. Often, he was just playing, but then, some people thought knives to be very serious toys. One can only conclude these same people thought getting the shakes was an appropriate reaction to any kind of stress.

Gathering in his knife, Cheyenne said,

"Old man, I'm looking for a fellow with a patch over his eye. He thinks he's some kind of pistolero. Tell me where I can find him and you'll see tomorrow. If you don't tell me, it's going to get real awkward."

"Mister, you are looking for poison."

"Maybe, but I must find him."

"Is he friend or enemy?"

In a flash, Cheyenne cut the old man's left nostril and had the scalpel sharp blade point in his right one.

"Patch, Patch, Patch, for Chrisake. Every one calls him Patch."

"I know that, you idiot. Where is he?"

Feeling pressure of the blade on his other nostril, he screamed,

"I'll tell ya, I'll tell ya."

"He's probably with the Mex gal at the edge of town. Last building at the end of the block."

The old boy made it sound like it was a long way. Perhaps it was, for him. He probably hadn't been there in years. From the look of it, neither had anyone else.

Cheyenne left his horse where he was and walked to the end of the block. Patch and the girl might be together and he didn't want to hurt the girl, so on cat feet he Injuned up to the open window and listened. Patch was grousing about his last job, the Indian raid, calling it "The Devil's Work" and how the pay was not worth it. To the girl, the guy sounded as though he were getting a conscience and showing some remorse. To Cheyenne, he sounded like a bullshitter.

Williams said,

"Over here."

The man turned and drew. Cheyenne threw the big knife with such force the big blade entered the man's head in the middle of his nose and the point came out the back of his head by an inch or two. Mr. Fancy Eye Patch fired and dropped. In the process, he shot off his own kneecap. Cheyenne, remorseless, retrieved his knife and branded the corpse with a big W.

"Sorry you had to see that Miss. Uh, Miss?" Miss?"

The girl was in shock. Cheyenne gave her some whiskey. She coughed and came around. Cheyenne walked her outside into the sunshine. She looked like the local, seedier than usual some-time hooker. The gods had not been kind to this girl. She was dirty, disheveled, and barefooted. Her hair was a mess and her dress was a rag.

"You got any kin in this town, Miss?"

"They rode off and left me about four days ago."

"What direction?"

She pointed west along the road.

"Where do you stay?"

"Wherever."

"When did you eat last?"

She glared at him.

"You just killed my meal ticket. He bought me breakfast at the café around seven this morning."

"That was hours ago. Come with me."

"I don't want to go back to town. The men stared at me and the women weren't nice to me."

"Here, try some of this jerky." Cheyenne walked back to get his horse and the girl followed at a distance. Then they walked toward a near-by stream. When they got there, he threw her in the water. Then he threw her some soap.

She came up sputtering, then bitched and swore with more than some degree of skill. Cheyenne was sure she had been taught by pros. He noticed she still had the beef-jerky. He smiled and said,

"You can come out when you are clean. Take off that rag you are wearing and throw it away."

Then he sat on the ground, leaned against a willow tree trunk on the stream bank to watch, and drink a little whiskey.

"I don't have to do anything you say."

"Yes, you do, until you are clean, or until you are rescued by some wandering knight who specializes in saving fair damsels from rogues like me."

She smiled for the first time, took off her dress, tossed it out into the stream and watched it slowly float away, a quiet ritual of her own.

Cheyenne said,

"Botticelli's "Birth of Venus."

She surprised him when she countered,

"Something like that."

"Where did you learn of the Renaissance painter?"

"I was raised in Italy. There one grows up with great painting all around."

"Then are you not Mexican, but Italian?"

"I am mostly English and Irish with some Italian thrown in."

The girl, nude, hip deep in the stream, was scrubbing her long, beautiful, raven hair. She accidentally put soap on the end of her nose while trying to keep it out of her eyes. Though comical, she was still beautiful. They were in the middle of nowhere and yet here they were talking of great painting, as if they were in someone's drawing room.

Cheyenne, being a sensible traveler, was happily indulging in the great scenery the girl provided and something for the palate as well; he was sipping whiskey and thoroughly enjoying himself. At least, the girl wasn't shy.

"Lady, what the hell are you doing in this dump?"

"It's a long story."

"I'm sure it is. I have time."

"I don't know you well enough."

"More to the point, what the hell am I doing here?" He asked, rhetorically.

Still scrubbing, she said,

"Perhaps you were hungry too."

"Hungry? I can find food when there isn't any. This is my kind of country. What would you like to eat? I'll hunt for us."

"For me, too?"

"Yes, of course."

Cheyenne decided to take a bath as well. Peeling off his clothes, but still wearing two knives strapped to his body, he waded in and swam for a moment. When he was close, she handed him the soap.

"If you are the knight you spoke of, perhaps you can provide me with what I am to wear when I get out of this stream."

She had been in the cool stream about fifteen minutes and was beginning to shiver. He saw her chill bumps.

"Yes, I can. I'll get you one of my shirts."

In a few minutes and after his quick bath, Cheyenne walked to his horse, opened his saddlebag and removed a nearly new, buckskin shirt. As the girl came out of the water, he noted that even though all of her ribs showed, she was otherwise rather shapely and had very nice legs. The girl was a mystery and Cheyenne was intrigued.

Out of the water, they sun dried and dressed. He tossed her the shirt and watched her put it on. It fit her like a baggy shroud and she didn't have any hands. The ludicrous costume was quite short; enough to be very provocative, and therefore was really quite charming.

"How do I look?"

"Very leggy."

"Is that bad?" she asked, knowing perfectly well, it wasn't and that he liked it.

They both smiled. He gave her a rawhide thong to use as a belt and helped her roll up her sleeves until she had hands again.

"Now what," she asked.

"Now we hunt."

Cheyenne mounted up and then offered his hand and a stirrup to her. As she swung up behind him he looked at those tantalizing legs and rolled his eyes upward. She noticed, smiled inwardly liking his reaction, but didn't say anything.

"Hang on."

They cantered a short way to the edge of the timber. The day was moving toward dusk and the critters would be out. It wasn't long before they saw a few deer. They climbed down, tied the horse, and taking his bow and arrows, sneaked up on their quarry. Cheyenne, with one shot, brought down a young deer. He gutted the beast in minutes. Then they rode slowly back to the stream, the carcass flopping behind the girl with every step.

Williams built a roasting fire and threw on a haunch. Walking around together, he found wild onions and cut two green willow sticks. When they returned, he sliced two large steaks, put them on the willow sticks and placed the sticks in the ground so the steaks were over the glowing coals. He took out the whiskey and water, gave her a cup and sat down to wait for the steaks to broil. Pouring her a little booze, he said,

"Tell me about yourself."

He leaned against a tree and got comfortable. They both had a sip and waited. The girl was off in her memory bank, gathering her thoughts. She finally gave him a long look, and began with,

"My father was a most unusual man, in some ways rather like you are. He was an adventurer. He was handsome, capable, and fearless.

"He had several businesses in the South, something in San Francisco, and later he acquired a cattle ranch somewhere west of here. He married an eastern girl who had been educated in Europe. My parents separated, and when the Civil War started, mother and I were living in England. The winters were quite cold there, so when I was nine we moved to Italy. We lived in several places, but mostly in Venizia, what you call Venice. Mother said we had merely moved from the Crowned Lion, the symbol of the British Empire, to the Winged Lion, the symbol of Venice."

"My father was later killed in that dreadful war, so Mother decided to stay on in Italy. Then, about six months ago, she died in the influenza epidemic, and I came here to claim the ranch. As far as I know, it is still operating and I think it is fairly sizeable. There is a law firm in San Francisco that has handled all of my father's business things for years. I think they are related somehow: Murdock and Schafer. The reason I remember is that they sent us a check every month, even though we didn't need it. Mother had her own money."

"What's your name, girl?"

"I'm Morgan Murdock. What's yours?"

"Cheyenne Williams."

She smiled prettily and held out her hand.

"It's nice to meet you, Mr. Cheyenne Williams."

He shook her hand, and felt the strong grip; he liked this girl.

"Let's eat. Then you can tell me how you ended up in that rat-hole town with one of the world's most evil men. I suppose that is another long story?"

"Not very. I arrived in New Orleans by ship and took the train to and through western Kansas. I hired a guide, Patch, and his man and horses, to take me the rest of the way. They brought me here to where you found me. They didn't molest me, but they did take everything I had including my clothes. I bathed in this same stream a week ago. When I came out, I was naked and had no clothes or possessions. I supposed it was meant to be a perverse joke. I went to that dingy labyrinth after dark, where you found me, and luckily found that filthy dress. I managed to stay out of sight for four days. Then I guess they changed their minds, because Patch came back for me, just before you showed up. Patch thought the whole incident very funny. I told him he was fired and he thought that was also very funny. He thought he was then in charge and that I had to do as he said."

"He told me he would see me to the ranch and if it was as he thought it might be, then we were to marry and he would take charge of it. He said if I didn't cooperate, he would give me to his man. The guy was such a beast, I readily agreed. You never saw an uglier brute."

"Patch was weird about women. He seemed indifferent to me. His man was even stranger. Sometimes, when he watched me, he would literally drool. He was disgusting. I don't think he cared about the ranch, but when he looked at me, I felt as I imagine a mouse would feel when caught by a large, heinous cat."

"Where is this beast now?"

"He's probably lurking around here somewhere, though I haven't seen our horses."

"Where did you last see him and how long ago was that"?

"Right here, four days ago."

The fresh meat and generous portions of scotch made for a wonderful picnic. Morgan Murdock felt great and looked even better in her new, shorty, buckskin dress. She was so leggy Cheyenne had to avert his eyes just to think straight.

Later, looking at the ground, Cheyenne questioned her further.

"You saw that gorilla right here?"

"No. The horses were over by that hitch rail and we mounted up there after buying a few essentials at the general store."

"Let's go have a look."

Cheyenne walked around the area and asked,

"Did any of the horses have a problem with their feet?"

"I heard Patch discussing the shoe of one of the animals, but I don't recall what it was about."

Looking further, Cheyenne found an unusual shoe print. There was a steel plate across the back part of the shoe. He could follow that print to the moon, but he wasn't sure if the shoe belonged to one of the girl's horses or to another.

"Come on, little lady, let's get you something to ride."

They walked back to the livery and Cheyenne bought one of the horses that he had sold the livery stable owner earlier. The man liked making a quick profit and was very pleased. Cheyenne asked,

"Have you seen a big, ugly, brute of a man, wandering around your town this morning?"

"As a matter of fact, I did see such a person awhile ago. He left his horse here and wandered on down the street. That fella is one you'd remember."

"Show me the horse."

"It's that black over there."

Cheyenne led the girl over to the critter.

"Is that one of your horses?"

"Yes, I bought all of the horses, except the one Patch was riding."

"That means the bad guy is still in town. If we leave now maybe we can lose him. He's not on my list so we won't bother with him unless he follows us. Go in there and get some new clothes for the ride."

Cheyenne gave Morgan some money, crossed the main drag to a store, found a window so he could watch the street, and settled down to wait. He knew the bad guy was after the girl. Sure enough, the big slob had been watching them, and saw Cheyenne and the girl separate. When Morgan went into the general store to get outfitted, he followed her.

Curious to see just how the "big gorilla" intended to abduct the girl, Cheyenne entered the store from the rear. When he arrived, he found the lady store-owner had been conked on the head, and she was out like a light. She would have a large bump on her head, but she would eventually be all right. Cheyenne quietly went through the hall and found that the big man had gagged Morgan's mouth and he was busy tying her wrists together.

"That's enough." Cheyenne said.

The man turned, glaring a look of venomous hatred. He started to lift his pistol, then saw the huge knife in his chest, was astonished, started to rise, and his lights went out. He fell with the same heavy crash of any all-purpose, three hundred and forty pound slob.

As far as Cheyenne knew, the big ugly beast had not been on the raid at the Indian village, but he did try to abduct a lady, and for our hero, that was more than enough to put the man's name on his list of the short lived. Cheyenne Williams took a very dim view of people who tried to do harm to any of his friends. He had spent a good part of the last several years being a "knight of the plains." Injustice angered him wherever he found it, but especially so if a girl type was involved; even more so if she was pretty.

Williams put his big foot on the dead man's chest, grabbed his knife and pulled hard. There was a ghastly sucking sound, and for the second time that day, Cheyenne helped the girl through her shock. He removed the gag and with a little more whiskey, she recovered and asked,

"Do you do this sort of thing all of the time, or just when you begin to get bored?"

He smiled, liking her spunk and said,

"I only make war on the bad guys and besides, the West has far too many bad men in it, any way. Those bastards won't be missed, not by the decent people, anyway, and probably not even by their own kind. I only wish I could have gotten to all of them sooner. The only thing any of that breed is good for, is food for the vultures. We didn't want that gorilla following us and I feel much better knowing that he is safely put away."

"Following us where?"

"First we'll find your horses, then we'll go on to your ranch to get you situated. I have one little thing to do on the way, but that shouldn't take long."

"Do I have any say in this?"

"No, not really, because I can't trust anyone else to get you there safely and in this country you are helpless. Maybe, by the time we get to your ranch, you will be better prepared to look after yourself."

"What do you mean?"

"Do you know how to shoot a pistol?"

"No."

I'll show you how to shoot, and later, how to throw a knife, if we have time. The knife takes longer. Both skills take a lot of practice. I prefer the knife. It is always as reliable as your skill. Knives are great up close. They're quiet, and they never miss-fire as pistols sometimes do."

"I'll buy some more ammo and we can be on our way."

The girl went for the black horse, and saw the macabre sight. The two hanging forms were gathering flies. She gulped, took a deep breath, proceeded to find her horse and led him out of there.

The big black was gentle as a lamb and strong as a bull. He had carried the big slob effortlessly. He could easily carry this girl half way around the world. They liked each other immediately.

Moments later, they met in the middle of the street and mounted up. The girl was strong. She reached for the saddle horn with both hands, then pulled herself up to where she could step into the stirrup and swung aboard. The two of them rode out at an easy trot with Cheyenne leading a packhorse. They both noticed the commotion around the livery stable as they rode away. Cheyenne thought to himself that the town of slow thinkers had finally awakened with about the same glacial speed as the two old guys had moved. He figured those hanging boys were likely to get rather rank before anyone in that burg could figure out how to cut them down. He had seen no one strong enough to lift them down, nor any one tall enough to reach to where the rope was tied. He smiled at the thought.

CHAPTER TEN

Cheyenne rode beside the girl. He liked looking at her and mused to himself about his altruism. Would he have helped her if she had been ugly? Nah! He hadn't become that selfless, not yet. Well, maybe. Perhaps, one day, he might. He knew he had changed some. Since helping Zero Smith in the Pinedale War, he figured he was no longer the most selfish man on the planet. Close, but not the most selfish man. He wondered whether he was weakening. Doing what one wants, when, where, how and as often as one wants was his idea of the perfect way to go through life, and he had. Of course other people objected on occasion, and when they did, he figured it helped to keep him sharp.

At the moment, his feeling of altruism toward the girl was suspect. She had "supplies" written all over her, but this feeling was more than that. He figured if he didn't get laid, he would probably still help her. This was a very unusual behavior for our hero and he was sure it required some thought.

Now, he had the problem of where to leave the girl while he dealt with the last few names on his list. The man he was following was said to be a gambler and Cheyenne figured that meant traveling to towns big enough to put six or eight men around each of several tables at the same time. The only town nearby that could meet that requirement, was a place called Twin Falls. It was farther west on the Snake River. The town was likely to have a hotel, but it was also likely to have a sheriff. The girl could stay in the hotel and he would try to stay away from the sheriff. With that thought in mind, he settled down to enjoy what he estimated to be a five-day trip.

The trail led to a quiet place along the river and they stopped for lunch. It was plain fare, but adequate. They had a quick swim accompanied by several longing looks at each other, but nothing more, dressed and rode out. Cheyenne wasn't at all sure of this girl. He decided to wait and let her make the first move.

The ride was pleasant and the scenery interesting. That afternoon they came to a wooded grove and halted, climbing down to take a breather. It was warm. There were some high brush and several large shade trees.

"Would you like to shoot now?"

"Yes, I think so."

"Let's go over to that clay bank. Here, we are too close to the horses. See that small bush growing out of the bank? Aim for the base of it."

He removed the shells and handed her one of his pistols, butt first.

She was surprised at how heavy it was. He showed her how to pull the hammer back with her thumb and how to gently squeeze the trigger. She let the gun hang at her side and then raised it and fired at the bush. She did that many times. Cheyenne handed her some lamb's wool to put in her ears, then reloaded the pistol.

"Watch."

He fired three times. The noise was deafening. A cloud of dust burst up from the base of the bush in the clay bank. She saw where each bullet had struck.

Cheyenne reloaded, and standing behind her, handed her the big Colt.

"Now you try it, but don't touch the trigger until you are ready to fire." As the girl raised her hand to fire he admonished her to hang on tightly. POWWW, and the big pistol bucked. There was a visible puff of dust on the clay bank not far from the bush.

She giggled with excitement.

"Now try it again."

He showed her how to sight down the barrel with one eye and then told her to keep both eyes open.

"Just point and fire."

she fired. This time she was close to the bush. She continued to fire the remaining four bullets.

Next he showed her how to reload and how to exchange cylinders. Then he gave her several extra loaded cylinders. She fired up a storm. She did it again, and again.

"I'm going to have a look around. Keep practicing, and try to keep track of how many times you dust that little bush."

When he left, Morgan felt very alone, but she discovered to her surprise, the big Colt .44 gave her a sense of comfort. She continued to practice with even more determination.

Cheyenne could hear the girl "shooting up a storm;" there was the grim possibility that others could too. He rode in a large circle. He heard one round twang off a tree and knew she had fired prematurely. The clay bank was only slightly higher than he was on horseback. He decided to stay out until she quit firing. When she did, he called out to her, and rode in.

He found her in a sweat, with a sore wrist.

"I hit the bush about twenty times and when I missed it, I was still close, particularly toward the last. It's hard work, but it's fun," she exclaimed.

"It was easier when I used both hands to steady my aim."

"Then use both hands when you get tired."

"What?"

He walked to her and removed the lamb's wool from her ears, remembering a time when his grandfather had done the same thing to him, and for the same reason.

He repeated the both hands bit.

"You did very well. I watched from back there."

The girl swelled with pride and flashed a great big smile.

"I will get you a gun that is more your size and you'll find it much easier to shoot." He applied a smelly gunk to her wrist.

"There. You are ruined socially for awhile, but your wrist will feel better in the morning."

"What is this awful stuff?"

"You don't want to know. We'll move over to the river again and you can rest. It's only a few miles from here."

They stopped at another grassy meadow in the shade of huge old cottonwood trees at the edge of the river. They found a back eddy in the stream that was deep enough for swimming and they both went in. She noticed that Cheyenne always swam with at least one knife and inquired, why. He answered with,

"This is rough country."

What he really meant was, this was wonderful country, but that it was populated with every kind of scoundrel: murderers and brigands, rapists and thieves, deserters from both sides of the war, and just not nice people in general. Some of them were the same kind of men who were on his list, the kind of men he was hunting.

He resented these unpleasant thoughts coming into his mind at a time like this, but knew himself to be ever wary, always on guard. Out here the careless died.

He swam closer to her and quietly suggested she keep her voice down and to swim only in the shadows.

"I didn't see any thing on the ride, but one can't be too careful."

In a short while he got out of the water and put on his big knife and gun belt; no clothes, just his knife and gun belt. He was already wearing the other knife. Then he stood in the sun to dry. In a little while she got out and walked toward him. He wasn't sure just how long he could wait for her to make the first move, when to his surprise, she did. She walked up to him, put her arms around his neck and her body into his, and gave him a great big kiss.

"You are so beautiful," she said.

"I was about to say the same thing about you."

Cheyenne knew he was looking at "supplies," and was very pleased. He led her to his bedroll and they both sat down. He poured whiskey and discovered she was randy and ready. A short while later she lowered herself down on to him, her eyes rolled back, until just the whites of her eyes showed. It was a little scary, but Cheyenne had seen this behavior before. He knew she had spaced out. She really didn't know where she was, or with whom. He was not offended, but quite the contrary, he was pleased to raise her to such an extraordinary high. She became nearly mute. This girl could concentrate. Awhile later, she occasionally said,

"Ahh,"

And again,

"Ahhh."

And still again,

"Ahhhh."

She groaned loudly and then mouthed soundless whispers.

Her breathing speeded up and slowed only to speed up again.

She seemed tireless, even though she had climaxed repeatedly. Cheyenne was very pleased with his new "supplies." Two hours later, and after a short rest, he was propped up on his bedroll, resting his head on his saddle. She had her head on his chest. He put his hand on her head, and pushed slightly. She slid down his frame to answer the question he didn't ask.

CHAPTER ELEVEN

The next day at dawn they packed for the trail again.

The girl was bright eyed and cheerful and Cheyenne was being his usual early morning grouch. He managed to catch the horses and to load the packhorse. When he finished loading the panniers and had them well secured, he looked across the campground and found an item or two that occasionally managed to escape being packed, so he left them. Scowling, he mounted up and rode out. The girl picked up the items without him knowing it, and stored them in her saddlebags. She would surprise him with them later. She smiled to herself and was pleased. She liked this big grouchy bear and had sense enough to be quiet until he came out of his "early morning dismal."

It was a very pleasant morning with the sun and the critters all doing their sun and critter things.

The sun was warming the earth and she saw several antelope, a rabbit, and a great variety of birds all going about their business of living in this beautiful place. The grass was thick, green and healthy. Cheyenne knew that cattle would thrive here.

It was so pleasant a morning, even the grouch came around in a couple of hours, and they stopped along the trail to make coffee and have a bite to eat. He built the fire and she prepared the food.

It was the first time they had divided the work along customary sexual lines. It gave him a slight tug on his heartstrings. He knew she was a keeper, but for whom? He also knew that he was always in love with the girl he was with, a condition that had been his salvation and at the same time, a major dilemma for much of his adult life. He had managed to remain single because of it. He wasn't at all sure it was the best way, but he was reasonably sure that it was his way.

After coffee, they moved on until mid-day, when they found a nice spot and lunched, had a nap, a swim, and each other. It was a perfect time.

Morgan finally said,

"This is so much fun, I don't care if we ever get to the ranch or to anywhere."

"You will if it rains."

Cheyenne could feel moisture in the air and he saw the clouds were gathering.

"The wind is freshening, and look at the horses. They can feel the storm coming. We had better find some shelter."

She looked around at the great empty space and said,

"Lots of luck."

"Follow me."

They saddled, mounted up and Cheyenne kicked the big horse into a canter. They were on high flat ground and he headed them down into a draw among some low hills. There was a lazy stream in the bottom, meandering along.

Morgan liked the spot and said so. Cheyenne disagreed.

"We can't stay here. Ride to higher ground. That little stream could turn into a raging river in a few minutes."

Cheyenne found a thick cottonwood grove on higher ground and stopped. The mid-day sky grew very dark. The air was full of static electricity. Then the lightning flashed and was followed by heavy cracks of thunder that rolled across the land. They were almost the same conditions that produce St. Elmo's fire. Lightning struck an old tree and caused it to explode as if dynamited. Large shards of deadly wood and bark went flying through the air, some of them four feet long. The next loud crack of crashing thunder seemed to be directly overhead.

He tied the horses, left the saddles on and hurriedly unpacked two large buffalo robes and three one-quarter robes. He tied a quarter robe over the head of each horse. The effect was to protect their eyes, to blindfold, and to calm them all at the same time. Then he gave a protective robe to the girl who was beginning to be pommeled by the hail. She immediately covered her head and hunkered down. Cheyenne grabbed her hand and led her to a space between two fallen trees. By then the wind was fierce. It blew ten times what it had only moments before, and bean size hail hammered the ground. The hail clattered against the tree trunks. It bounced every which-way, and sounded like someone throwing gravel on a thin board roof. The stuff would have hurt if they hadn't been protected under the heavy buffalo robes.

The wind increased and blew the hail sideways, down, and even up, at times. They hunkered down between the two large fallen trees and were fairly safe. They were protected from the sides by the trees and from the top by the robes. Then, after a few more minutes, the hail turned to a deluge of torrential rains. They watched safely from the higher ground, as the quiet little stream became a raging river. Volumes of muddy water careened around each curve in the stream bed, carrying debris from further up the stream. The water came with such force that it climbed the high bank of each turn in the stream. It angrily clawed away the heaped soil and carried it away like it was treasure.

Cheyenne had noticed all his life that the earth seemed to want to be flat. Some high hills, even during his lifetime, in a few places, had been washed away to a lesser mass, or, as with a few sand banks, eroded to nearly flat land. He didn't know the high Rocky Mountains were rising faster than they were being eroded away, or that they too, would eventually be eroded to round hills, like the Appalachian Mountains. Cheyenne thought the storm would be brief and it was. It lasted about thirty minutes and then it went capriciously on to disturb several other environs.

Most of the critters of the woods would successfully re-adjust. They saw two small rodents, which had taken refuge in a large tree, slowly climb down as the storm passed. There were nearly always a few casualties from such a storm. The casualties were mostly among dispossessed burrowing type critters. The coyotes, foxes, owls, hawks, bobcats, and a few other predators would feast for several days.

The two riders spent the rest of the day drying out and loafing around the fire. The sun was out in force, but it took awhile to warm the air after the storm. Cheyenne shook out more buffalo robes, his bedroll, and some whisky. Gradually things were bearable again. The girl just took off her clothes.

From the newly blown down leaves, she made a leaf crown for her head and put it on. Then she started on a leaf costume for herself. She managed to make a very short and provocative skirt from a great variety of leaves woven together.

"Should I do the rest?"

Then she answered her own question.

"Nah!"

So she teasingly walked around, flashing her beautiful and barely covered backside, her long beautiful legs, and her magnificent breasts until Cheyenne couldn't stand it any more. He led her to his bed role. She was wearing a very bright, pleased and triumphant smile.

Afterward, he said,

"Morgan, the forest nymph and coquette, all rolled into one great package."

She answered by saying.

"Shouldn't one aspire to greatness at something?"

"Girl, you have already met any girl's highest aspiration of womanhood very successfully, and I might add, any man's highest expectations as a lover with equal success. To put it succinctly, Morgan Murdock, you are one terrific lady."

She beamed back a big smile.

"I had fun making the costume for you. I must do it again sometime."

"Please do. I liked it. It was very effective," he said and smiled.

The girl beamed and said,

"Praise from the master."

CHAPTER TWELVE

Two days later Cheyenne and Morgan arrived at a way station of a newly established stagecoach line. At the way station, fresh teams replaced the tired horse teams. The stagecoach passengers were allowed to stretch their legs, eat, drink, visit the outhouse, and be on their way. Travel by stagecoach was certainly precarious. The travelers were often victimized by outlaws, harassed by Indians, slowed by the vast herds of buffalo, and even mauled by violent storms. Occasionally, they were victimized by several different causes all at the same time. Travelers were also prey to the inevitable dust that was kicked up by the four or six horse teams, and to the dust from the two front wheels' of their own coach on dry days, and to the dust of all four wheels, if there was a following wind.

Stagecoach passengers were also subject to spattering mud when it rained, and to mud puddles when they disembarked. Muddy boots were the norm for most of the spring and fall and a lady's dress was just the right length to drag through the mud and other assorted horribles left by a zillion animals when she walked. As if that weren't enough, the roads often featured zero maintenance and gut wrenching chuckholes. The remark, "Have a safe journey," was taken very seriously. Some passengers with good reason, called on their respective deities for additional help. Travel was always a bit dicey, but then so was life on the western frontier.

Cheyenne and the girl arrived well after the stagecoach had gone through. They stopped to rest their horses and to eat. The friendly hostler was kind to his horses and rude to the passengers, but Cheyenne and the girl were neither one, so he was friendly and loquacious. His friendliness may have been because Morgan was riding astride, and therefore wearing tight fitting long pants that showed off her lush round back side when she walked around. Even with riding clothes on, the girl was a great visual. Morgan could cheer up anyone's day.

Cheyenne asked a lot of questions of the old hostler and learned the location of the cow town on the girl's ranch. He also learned who was running it, and roughly the size of the big spread. The town was known as Murdock, the ranch was called the Big Murdock, and it was big, very big. It was about 300,000 contiguous acres, with plenty of good water and both valley and higher-up graze.

The brand was a large M placed on the right side of the cattle and a small M placed on the right hip of the horses.

The current operating manager was a thirty-year-old pistolero called Slade Colby. He was an obnoxious bastard who rode rough- shod over nearly everything around him. A malcontent who specialized in verbal abuse and intimidation, he backed it up with a modicum of gun skill. He spent a lot of time terrorizing the locals and, particularly, the young ladies of the nearby town. Naturally, Cheyenne hated him immediately.

After the way station, their first stop was the town of Murdock. The town was nothing special, but it did have a few of the essentials that make a western town. The first of these essentials was a whorehouse. The second essential was a bar and restaurant; third was a general store, and fourth and fifth were a combination hotel and restaurant, probably in the reverse order. Sixth was a gun shop where he bought Morgan a .38 caliber revolving six-gun. Seventh was a bank, and the remaining enterprises were debatable in terms of their placement on so arbitrary a list of essentials. There was a livery stable where one could buy, sell, trade, or stable a horse, rent a wagon, buggy and team, and get all of the news and gossip even when you didn't want it. After that came the bakery, then the haberdashery, and two more bars. A small shop sold snake oils of one kind or another, some from as far away as India, which naturally made the cures more effective, as they were shrouded in Middle Eastern myth and nonsense.

There was a good saddle shop that could outfit a cowhand. It featured clothes, ropes, bridles, quirts, whips, rain gear, harnesses, big hats, spurs, chaps, pointy boots and chewing tobacco. Last on the list was a church of unknown denomination, skippered by a suit, selling "fire and brimstone." His role in life was to try to scare the Hell out of nearly everybody, a practice at which he was less than successful. He labeled anything that looked like a good time, a sin.

Happiness, joy and laughter were all highly suspect conditions and probably the work of Satan. The poor man was convinced that gambling, liquor and loose women were the tools of the Devil and that he was called by God to save others from said great fun, other Satanic evils, and of course, from themselves. When Cheyenne heard this, he wondered where this clown studied his particular set of dialectics and vowed to be a shining example of everything the man was opposed to, and to give him the attention he deserved, which was none.

The town was called Murdock mostly, the locals said, because it was built as a supply place for the big ranch, which surrounded it. In fact, the ranch headquarters was still a long ride toward the northwest. The locals sometimes used the term "M town" for the town of Murdock and "the big M" to designate the ranch.

The name Murdock packed a lot of weight with the locals, or it would have, if there were any Murdocks left. Cheyenne learned these sterling bits of news from the gossip center of Murdock's known world, the hostler at the livery stable. The word about this guy was that if he didn't know about it, "it just hadn't happened yet."

Our two travelers moved into the hotel for two days and then planned to head out to the main ranch house. No rancher would build his house near large stock pens and neither had Murdock. He built his stock pens on open prairie before there was a town, not expecting a town to start up near by. The town blossomed as the ranch grew and prospered. Later, the town's people were told, "that's the smell of money," but money for whom? Perhaps a little of the money did trickle their way, but most of it went to the Murdock Cattle Company.

Over the years, the company thought it advisable to own most of the town, so they bought anything that came up for sale. Later, the Murdock people in San Francisco, with the help of the territorial governor, were instrumental in having the railroad, on it's way west, built right next to the town of Murdock. The railroad got some free dirt and the big M got easy access to shipping their cattle. More importantly, it also ended the long trail drives.

When Morgan Murdock rode into her town, she didn't know she actually owned about eighty-five per cent of the place, nor did she know that she owned all of the Murdock Cattle Company. She was, however, rather impressed with what her father had accomplished in a fairly brief period.

//////

Cheyenne was thinking. He was propped up on the bed in their hotel room, his Apache boots off, barefooted, with whiskey in hand. It took some serious doing to hold and operate a ranch the size of the Big Murdock. It seemed to Cheyenne that it might be rather easy for a fast gun to take over the operation if none of the Murdock family was paying attention.

He decided to wire Morgan's people in San Francisco, explain Morgan's arrival at the ranch town, and to please advise, etc. While they waited for a reply, the girl couldn't have been happier. Her life was just one great big giggle. Cheyenne was having a difficult time trying to be serious. They needed more information from the locals, the ranch management people, and the San Francisco money controllers. He wired everybody. He discovered who the major players were in the town, on the ranch and in San Francisco, and then he sharpened his knives.

"Will that be necessary?"

"You never can tell, girl, but it's a big enough pot for the greedy players to get real serious and very nasty. We are likely to rattle some cages before we're through. Your two-gun pistolero has what amounts to a small army on his payroll. He may not want to step down so easily. We'll know more when your man from San Francisco arrives. It's up to him to explain just what your position is.

And, of course, you must prove who you are to his satisfaction. Can you do that?"

"I think so."

"Good, how about lunch?"

She giggled, gave him a hungry look that had nothing to do with food and said,

"Do you mean me or the real thing?"

"Woman, you are the real thing."

CHAPTER THIRTEEN

They romped through the day, missed lunch, and ordered a bath sent up. The hotel's pride and joy was a large copper tub, which was big enough for both of them at the same time.

She had champagne, soapsuds and mischief. Because of her mischief, he had a soggy cigar and whisky.

//////

If the girl was who she said she was, he vowed to see that this little "meek," would inherit her part of the earth. He intended to make it very difficult for any people who wanted to steal her property. She would inherit as a Murdock, though she didn't know it yet, all 300,000 acres of a working cattle ranch,

85% of a town, and several assorted small businesses.

He decided to have a council of war, a strategy session of about twenty minutes, in which he would explain to her what he intended to do in the next few days. Then they would celebrate. They would make medicine, which sometimes meant each other; this was one Indian who had his priorities continuously in mind. He smiled as he contemplated a rewarding romp with her. He could hardly move from the last one, and he was already thinking about the next time. He knew he had a big appetite, but this was ridiculous.

They didn't dance around a fire and yell and scream, but they did dance around each other, while she screamed, moaned and eventually purred. He simply hung on. Their behavior wasn't sacrificial, but it was primitive and it certainly was a right-of-passage. He went from being angry, to being the proverbial lamb that had laid a lioness.

The next day, he decided that Morgan would stay put, but he would ride out to meet the "bad guys."

//////

Cheyenne put on his "I'm looking for a riding job" cowhand clothes, which meant a beater hat, torn this, frayed that, and with worn down heels, rode toward the ranch. As usual, he was fully armed.

Fully armed really meant that he was what his friend Todd called a "walking arsenal." He carried all of his usual stuff, but everything was out of sight except his pistol and his ever-present big knife. On his saddle he carried only his Winchester. The two Colt .44 saddle pistols usually holstered, one on each side of the saddle horn, were now rolled up and in his saddlebag. Cheyenne Williams was a slow fuse, lighted and ready for war.

//////

It wasn't long before he found two cowhands mending fence and asked them the way to the ranch headquarters.

They were a nasty pair and implied that being a "breed," he was wasting his time. He took one look at them and figured them for what they were, two very bigoted rustics. He said,

"I think I'll let the ramrod tell me that."

One of the men wanted to make an issue out of Cheyenne's statement, but the other one smiled with the eyes of a rattlesnake and calmed his sidekick. Cheyenne hadn't intended to ruffle anyone's feathers. He smiled back and rode on. He thought it prudent to let them live for the next several days. He reasoned it would be rather ballsy to ask for a job while he was leading saddle horses with two of the spread's dead cowhands draped over their saddles.

Cheyenne's English friend would have said, "Bad form." Williams smiled at the thought.

Cheyenne arrived looking like any cowhand, sought out the ramrod and asked for a riding job. The main man foreman was away and this ramrod was his Segundo. When that was made clear, there was the usual chat. He gave his name as Williams and then he was shown the bunkhouse where he chose an empty bunk and put away his gear. Cow camps were pretty much the same, though some were a little friendlier than others. There was nothing friendly about this place; there was tension here, the kind one could cut with a knife. Well, Cheyenne Williams certainly had the knives for it.

Cheyenne was hired and riding for the Murdock brand. They didn't know it, but they now had a fox in their hen house.

That evening, at chow time, he met most of the riders stationed at this location. He did not recognize any of the men, which he thought was just as well.

As usual, who did what was decided over breakfast. Williams was to ride with two other men; all three cowhands were to move bulls to a different area. One of the men was a fair hand with a whip, so he was elected to do the sticky stuff, but they were all issued whips, and told to do the best they could with them. Cheyenne was not unfamiliar with whips, but they were not his best toys.

The bulls were new arrivals and they were to join the ladies about ten miles away. Bulls being what they are don't drive well, and they usually don't take to each other, so the boys had their hands full. But with the whips popping and cracking they soon had the bulls' attention and they moved well enough. The men tried to encourage the bulls with a promise or two about meeting fancy ladies just over the rise. It seemed to work for a while. After the first mile, the pace slowed considerably and there were always one or two that wanted to go in some different direction. A couple more miles of that kind of whip action and the cowboys' arms would fall off. A few times the bulls turned to charge the horses and the whips sailed out to take some hair. One cantankerous critter had his nose cut with a whip before he shaped up. Most of the critters moved by just cracking the whips in the air, somewhere over their backsides.

The men bitched and moaned about twenty bulls being a job for ten riders, and they shouldn't have to move them so far, etc. When they got close to their destination, the wind came up and saved them. The bulls got the message on the wind and picked up the pace until, finally, some trotted toward the party. The three much-relieved cowhands pulled up their mounts on a rise and watched.

Most of the critters were greeted with a friendly reception and the rest were busy tweaking the interest of some of the other cows. Soon, the bulls would have their own harem. Cheyenne was sure the bulls had the best job on any ranch.

Without his asking, the one man Cheyenne was curious about became the topic of conversation between the other two men. It seemed the ranch manager/foreman, Colby, was not well liked by anyone in the entire world, but he was a shooter and a good one, so most people walked softly around this big ego. The men told Colby what he wanted to hear and laughed at his juvenile jokes.

Apparently, Colby had arrived one day and said that he was in charge of the entire Murdock operation. He showed a legal looking document to a few of the top people and the banker and then took over, just like that. For about four years after the death of Morgan Murdock's father, the ranch had practically run itself until Colby arrived. He had been around for just over a year and in that time Colby managed to hire shooters who would do his bidding. They were men who were more familiar with guns than cows. Once established, Colby had gradually let the ranch slide down into its present state.

//////

Cheyenne worked for another week at the usual riding jobs, but learned little; however, he did learn something about the current ramrod and that Slade Colby was despised by nearly everyone.

The little man from San Francisco, a Mr. Spencer, arrived and the three had a meeting at the hotel. Spencer had been with the law firm and Murdock Corporation for over thirty years, but hadn't seen Morgan in about five years. She had changed considerably since he had last seen her. He was sure she was who she said she was, but he asked a few questions anyway. He asked Morgan a few family questions, the date of her birthday, what present she received on her thirteenth birthday, on her fourteenth birthday, where she lived and what present she received upon graduating from her finishing school in Devonshire, England. He asked her to tell him which presents were from her father and which were from other members of the Murdock firm. Spencer had sent them all and her answers satisfied him that she was indeed Morgan Murdock and the rightful heir to the Murdock estate. He was pleasantly surprised to find that she had filled out so well and turned into a dazzling beauty in the interim.

The next day Spencer went to the nearby bar where he attempted to fire Colby and Colby shot him. He would recover because luckily, the bullet had passed through his right side above the hip. No bones were broken and the Doc was competent enough to do the repair job. He probed for the bullet and sewed up his patient. Spencer was hurt, but managed to wire San Francisco to cut off all funds to the Murdock ranch, put a hold on all Murdock money in the local bank, and to notify all creditors they would not be paid until further notice. Colby and his thugs were broke over night.

With the money supply depleted, the Colby followers dwindled finally to one slow brain shooter and a no-neck disciple. Cheyenne's primary problem was to keep Morgan and Mr. Spencer alive and unharmed until things settled down. When Colby's goons moved, Cheyenne was ready for them.

They confronted him midday in the saloon, with witnesses. It was a simple insult by the slow brain, who considered himself, a first class shooter. The shooter calmly pulled on his thin kid gloves as though he were about to go to work, and said,

"I don't like half breeds,"

He then squared away on Cheyenne Williams.

Biiiiiiiggg mistake!

He made his move, but was much too late and was surprised to find that he was wearing a huge knife in his guts. Then his lights went out. The other man drew and fired into the floor. When the smoke cleared, the onlookers saw two holes through the fellow's heart. Cheyenne retrieved his big knife, cleaned the blade on the dead man's jacket and then carved a W on the forehead of each victim. An unseen town Indian was working in the back when the ruckus started. He stayed long enough to see Williams carve the W mark on the forehead of one of the dead shooters, and then he silently slipped away to his horse. It looked to the locals as if the Murdock operation had a new main man and they were right.

Colby, now alone, was furious. He seethed, sulked, and sought solace in the bottle, until the bar cut him off. That was the last straw. Colby was frustrated. One day he was riding high, and the next day he was in the outhouse with the door locked from the outside. His world had caved in. He knew of the half breed, Cheyenne, but otherwise, didn't know whom to fight. He had no money to buy more good guns and his two best guns were six feet under, stoking the fires of Hell. He could no longer intimidate the merchants or the cowhands. He reasoned that if he put holes in a few people, it would probably make things worse. He couldn't fight the whole town.

At Cheyenne's suggestion, Spencer issued an edict that put a chill in the bones of every local and every rider that worked for the Murdock property. The edict placed Morgan Murdock in sole charge of all financial operations. She signed the checks or paid the cash, or it didn't get paid. The purpose was to insure her safety and it worked. Suddenly, she was treated with deference, care, and respect. The locals knew she was related by name, but they did not know she was the sole heir to the entire corporation. Neither did she.

The sagacious little man from San Francisco, though still bedridden, had great fun with all of that. He had met Morgan the day she was born and had been keeping an eye on her affairs ever since. Lawyer Spencer was even a silent partner in some Murdock ocean shipping ventures, but only a few people in the home office knew that. Spencer hired Cheyenne for a huge sum to look after Morgan Murdock day and night. Cheyenne agreed, but not for the money. He had his own money and said so.

"Even better." Spencer said, "Now, would you mind telling the doctor that I want to move back into the hotel? It's nothing personal, but their food is better than his cooking. By the way, do you have any whiskey?"

"Do the plains have buffalo?"

"What? Oh, yes, of course. Thank you."

Eyeing the small flask given him by Cheyenne, he tasted it rather gingerly,

"Bless me, I do believe this is scotch."

"Yes, sir. It sure is. And that's the last of it, I'm afraid."

"Nonsense, my boy. I have three whole bottles in my valise. I shall make you a present of two of them as soon as I get moved."

Cheyenne left to find two careful men to move Spencer's belongings, but on second thought, decided the treasure was much too valuable to be entrusted to two lethargic menials who were apt to be unreliable on their very best day. He therefore moved Spencer's belongings himself. There were only two items: a medium sized steamer trunk and the treasure-trove valise. Cheyenne Williams handled the steamer trunk as though it were weightless and the valise as if it were liquid gold. The effects were moved in moments.

After Cheyenne locked the hotel room door, he went to help Spencer move back to the hotel. With the good doctor in command and on one side of Spencer and Cheyenne Williams on the other, the three men charged across the perilous street; the little man's feet sometimes peddling in the air dodging riders, buggies, and shouting teamsters with their four horse teams and wagons. They were shouted and cursed at in several languages, but all three managed to arrive safely intact at the hotel for their expected reward. For good scotch whiskey, Cheyenne would have stopped all of the traffic in the entire town, to insure that the little fellow arrived safely. After all, Spencer had the key to the valise that held the "aged in the barrel," liquid gold.

Spencer's wound was still very tender, but he managed a smile as the good people helped to once again prop him up in his hotel bed. That done, he asked for scotch. Cheyenne, using Spencer's key, found the treasured stuff and poured them all a sizable jolt. It was old, smooth, and good.

"Just what the doctor didn't order!" exclaimed Spencer.

"Gentlemen, to your health," offered the doctor. The three men drank solemnly, each man with his own thoughts.

"Gentlemen, to my new boss, Miss Morgan Murdock, a lady who is full of surprises," toasted Cheyenne.

"Did I hear my name being mentioned?" Morgan asked, as she arrived.

"You did indeed, pretty lady," remarked Cheyenne. "Care to join us in a small celebration?" and he poured her a sizable amount of the good stuff.

"What's the occasion?"

"Spencer has just moved back into your hotel."

"What do you mean, my hotel?"

Spencer broke in with,

"Morgan perhaps you had better sit down."

He patted his bed. She sat at the foot of the bed, looking puzzled as Cheyenne handed her a drink.

Spencer continued,

"Morgan, your father was a very, very clever business man. Everything he touched turned to gold. He had several partners over the years, but they are all dead now and so are all of their heirs. Brandenburg died last year of a heart problem, and his two sons were killed in the war."

"Schafer was an orphan and never married. I am an equal partner in the ocean shipping freight operations. I also have been the general manager of all of the companies for many years, and I, too, am without an heir. So you see, little girl, why we have kept such a close eye on you. When we lost you on the Kansas plains, I was extremely worried for your safety. When I was told that Cheyenne Williams found you, I was greatly relieved, and very much amused. Apparently you were wearing a disgusting cast off rag of a dress, and looked like a prairie waif. Morgan, you own three very large textile mills and many women's clothing stores."

"I knew you were no longer a child, but I had not expected you to turn into such a fancy lady. Naturally, I am very well pleased. You are all that's left of what I considered to be my family."

"Your father helped me through a very difficult time when my wife died. I let things go to hell until he kicked my backside. I finally came out of it, and it's been onward and upward ever since."

By this time everyone was sitting down. Cheyenne poured another round for each of them. The room was silent for a moment until Morgan asked in the barest whisper,

"Just how many companies do I own?"

The room was quiet with all eyes suddenly glued on Spencer. Spencer had been anticipating this moment for years. Each time he had made a new and successful acquisition of another business, he thought how pleased Morgan would be when he told her. At last, the moment had arrived. He hadn't expected to be bed ridden or shot full of holes, but this was the place and now was the time.

"Child", he said, with a great twinkle in his eye, "you own exactly one hundred and six separate and prosperous companies, plus buckets of stocks issued on companies that we do not own. Morgan Murdock, you, I'm happy to say, are one of the wealthiest women in the country."

Then he added, as if talking about her age,

"But I would continue to keep that a secret, if I were you."

"The fact is, my dear, that you are the sole surviving heir to everything with a Murdock stamp on it, and to many companies that do not carry the Murdock name."

Morgan was speechless as the information sank in. Mouths gaped and then grinned, then laughed. Finally, Morgan leaped up and squealed, then laughed, then cried, then she spun around and hugged Spencer, gave him a big kiss, and hugged him again.

"Wow."

Then she hugged each man in turn. It was the happiest day in the lives of two of the people, and one of the happiest days in the lives of the other two.

Spencer, now fifty-five, grimaced with pain at her zeal as she hugged and kissed him, and still thought it the best thing that had happened to him in his later life. He had known Morgan as a little girl, had been to her christening, witnessed her graduation from the eighth grade, from a secondary private school, and finally he was there for her graduation from Miss Wright's College and Finishing School for Young Ladies in Devonshire, England. He was the best friend and partner of her father, an adopted uncle to her, and a long time family friend. He was also her godfather, legal advisor and guardian of her fortune, a duty and noble calling, he administered and protected with the same zeal that Saint Peter guarded the Gates of Heaven.

If asked, Spencer was reasonably sure that he had made more money than Saint Peter, but admittedly, he had not saved any souls. From his view, why bother if there were no money in it? It was difficult to figure compound interest on such an intangible.

Spencer knew that making money was the one thing at which he excelled and he was delighted to have done so well in the name of the Murdock Trusts for Miss Morgan Murdock. She was the nearest thing he would ever have to a daughter, and he valued their relationship and friendship above everything else. Well, maybe not everything else, but he was sure that their friendship ran a close second to money.

His role as legal guardian was brief and never exercised because six months after her mother died, Morgan reached her majority and came of legal age. Just then, she had called him "Spencer" as she so often had as a little girl, and when she did, he beamed. Everyone called him "Spencer," but somehow when she said his name, it was different; it always made him feel good. It was a happy time for them all.

The girl exclaimed, "Since, I have all of this money, I want to give a wonderful dinner party. We'll have lots of fine food and the best champagne available!"

She looked at Cheyenne, questioning. He nodded that it could probably be done, even in that burg. After all, she was this week's all-purpose goddess/queen. She could make it happen. And if she couldn't, then he sure as hell could! Then he softened as he thought to himself that he wouldn't kill horses just to get champagne, even for one of the greatest bedroom artists of western civilization: the incomparable Miss Morgan Murdock.

Fortunately, the hotel did have champagne and they had their party, which was later followed by a smaller party of just two guests. Cheyenne Williams was proven correct; Morgan Murdock was indeed, incomparable.

CHAPTER FOURTEEN

Williams lazed around the town of Murdock for a few more days. They saw Spencer off on the train to San Francisco to go back and count his money, and their world returned to being only slightly abnormal. The town of Murdock slowly came to grips with the fact that it had a new boss. The money was still withheld and Morgan ignored the complaints of the populace. When one or two of the locals became difficult, Cheyenne put lumps, plural, on their heads.

Finally, Morgan called for a town meeting. When they all appeared, she told them the town was a dump. She told them there would be no money until it was cleaned up. They were to fix this and repair that, pick up every piece of trash, paper and broken this and rusty that, and haul them to a designated ravine dumpsite. She wanted the town cleaned up now. The people had four days to complete the task.

If they didn't want to do that, she would close down her businesses, which really meant eighty five percent of the town, and move out to the ranch. There would be no more money and the place would become a ghost town. The only thing left would be the shipping-pens. If they did decide to clean up their town, she would turn on the money flow, and she would move the shipping-pens about two miles down the railroad tracks to get the smell and most of the flies out of town.

Morgan stated, "Come see me in four days. I'll be in the hotel."

Morgan and Cheyenne returned to their rooms and opened some more champagne. They clinked glasses and Morgan twirled around, flaring her skirt, showing Cheyenne her shapely legs and said,

"Here's to playing God."

"You were good out there. They believed you and will work on your suggestions."

"My father once said, "we each need our ass kicked once in a while and when you give orders, do it as though you expect the orders to be obeyed. Out there, I did both. We'll see what happens."

"Now," she said, "Mr. Cheyenne Williams, if you are willing, for the next few days, I'm going to keep you in this bed and have my way with you." They both smiled, and she fulfilled her promise.

//////

Four days later she inspected the town and called the people together. She suggested they elect a mayor and a town council and run the place democratically. Very few knew what that meant. She explained how it worked, and then they elected a sheriff. Cheyenne thought they elected a good one.

She put the mayor and the sheriff on the town's payroll, not hers. She appointed a temporary town council, which was above the mayor and the sheriff to oversee the progress of the town until they could elect a council of their own.

Next, she gave the bank a letter of credit for a large amount and the town was back in business. The town was to be subsidized by the working cattle ranch, the same as always, but there would be money for schools and civic improvements.

Morgan took the mayor and the town council aside and suggested they hire people immediately to plant trees on the main street, big trees on both sides of the street for shade and beauty. She wanted flowers planted in beds, in pots, or in half barrels in front of every store. They were to send her the bill. She wanted this town to be something they could all be proud of. She warned them again that if they didn't take good care of their town, she would come back and move everything she owned out to the ranch and they would be left with a ghost town.

"I'll come back in two weeks to see how things are going."

Then she moved out to the ranch. Cheyenne went with her. He put her belongings in a buggy and tied their horses to the back. The drive out was pleasant and it allowed them to get a good look at a small area of the big spread. They drove through some high rolling hills with vast views of the country. There were cattle everywhere, most with calves. It was very good looking cattle country.

Cheyenne pointed out the neglect he saw in a few animals: old cows, poor quality bulls that should have been steered, cancer eye, and one old girl with an udder that dragged on the ground. They were things the foreman should direct his people to work on as soon as possible. Soon it would be a fine ranch again, a place her father could be proud of.

//////

They camped overnight on the trail, had their dinner, a bottle of wine, and sat against trees to watch the sunset. The evening was warm and life was good. The euphoria lasted until just after midnight, when they were hammered by a sudden cloudburst; it poured buckets.

They scrambled to get their gear in the buggy and Cheyenne draped tarps around the inside to keep out most of the slanting rain and they just sat out the downpour under the canopy. After an hour, the rain had let up so Cheyenne hitched the horse to the buggy and they moved out. They were damp, but not cold, and they had a little whiskey to compete with the chill. They drove until the sun was well up and the day was warm. Then, they stopped to dry out and have a snooze. All of the wet stuff steamed. Their wet clothes were draped over tree limbs and both of them were in the buff.

By eleven o'clock in the morning, Cheyenne and Morgan were stretched out on a nearly dry blanket in the tall grass enjoying the many varieties of wildflowers, the vast, cloudless blue sky, the bird songs, and the company of each other. The hot sun made the world better than tolerable as they lazed through the hours while waiting for their things to dry. They filled their water bottles, picnicked, rubbed backs, drank some coffee and later some good wine, and just generally enjoyed life as they made the best of the slight interruption in their travels. The only sound was from a calf, far away, bawling for its mamma. A warm rising breeze danced across the prairie grass on its way to anywhere.

The ranch headquarters was not far away, perhaps five miles. When their things had dried, they gathered and packed them and proceeded on their way to the ranch headquarters. They assumed the reception might be difficult, and they expected the news of a new boss lady to have preceded them. They were right on both accounts.

CHAPTER FIFTEEN

When Morgan and Cheyenne arrived, they found the ranch to be trashed in many ways. Fence rails were down in places. There were broken wheels on wagons. They found a water trough pump with no handle, horses and cattle wandering in the main house yard and several cowhands seated on a bench in the sun playing cards. They were speculating about the new owner.

Morgan climbed out of the buggy and asked where the foreman was. She was ignored. Cheyenne climbed down out of the buggy and threw a knife into the upper gun arm of the biggest cowhand on the bench. What ever gun skill he may have had, vanished forever. Cheyenne quietly said,

"Where is the foreman of this ranch?"

A second cowhand pulled his iron and was shot through the heart. He dropped to his knees and fell forward with his face in the dirt.

"Anyone else?"

The people immediately paid attention and became more respectful. Cheyenne retrieved his big knife, wiped it on the chest of the man he'd cut, and said, once again,

"Who and where is the big auger of this place?"

The people were compliant and cooperative.

They pointed down the way to a small house near a stable.

Cheyenne and Morgan went to the indicated place. When they arrived, they found a man raping a cowhand's wife. They were in a small house just off the stable area. The woman was fighting, screaming and crying. It was obvious rape. Cheyenne put a knife in the bad guy's throat and pole-axed the second man on the head with his pistol barrel. The second man was out like a light and looked ludicrous lying on the floor with his pants at half-mast. Apparently he had been waiting his turn. Cheyenne disarmed the man in seconds, roped his feet together and hoisted the man up on an overhead stable beam to hang upside down. The fellow's head was about six feet from the ground. This would have to do until they could find a space that would serve as a jail.

They hadn't been there twenty minutes and the ranch needed four new employees.

Morgan walked to a high wagon and climbed up on it. She shouted to all of those who could hear her.

"Go and tell your families and your friends that I am here. I am the new owner of this ranch. Then come back." She pointed at an old man, and said,

"Send me the man who has been here the longest."

"Senorita, that is me. My name is Julio, I have been here from the beginning, fourteen years."

"My name is Morgan Murdock, and I am the new owner of this ranch."

"Senorita, I knew your father. He was a good man, not like these scum that your friend has killed. I am very happy to see you. We have prayed for your return."

"Will the people come?"

"Yes, Senorita, they will come, but you must be careful. A few people will not like the fact that you are here."

Cheyenne suggested that they get inside where they could not be bushwhacked, at least, not until she had presented her case to the people of the ranch, after which he thought it unlikely.

When the people were assembled, Morgan spoke to them.

"I am the daughter of Mr. Murdock. I am the new owner of the Murdock ranch. I am also the only person who can write your payroll checks. If anything happens to me there will be no more money for you. It's important that you understand that. Anyone who attempts to harm me is really taking away your paycheck. This ranch cannot even buy a bale of hay unless I sign for it. This place is disgraceful. I've stopped all money for the ranch until we clean it up and get it running properly again. I don't know who or where the foreman is but he is fired."

Julio explained, "Senorita, he was the rapist your friend killed."

Most of the people had not heard of the rape and death of Colby. They moaned and sighed with disbelief, and then they smiled and praised the Saints. Many were sure their prayers had been answered. Cheyenne was no saint, but he had apparently answered a few prayers. Their belief said their God moved in mysterious ways. Perhaps he did.

Morgan addressed the ranch people,

"Now, we need a new ranch foreman. I would like you to suggest names of men whom you think would make a good foreman for this ranch."

The same name came up many times, and the man was brought forward. He had been the foreman when the shooter with the phony documents had shown up and replaced him. Everyone agreed that Gonzales was a good man and that the others would work for him. Morgan agreed and doubled his salary. Everyone was very pleased. He was told that he could run the ranch as he chose, but he must first consult with her each morning about its operation. She explained to the foreman it was to help her learn the problems of the ranching business and to help her keep an eye on the money flow. Even Gonzales had no idea just how big the Murdock ranch actually was, nor the impact his job would have on the country.

Morgan chose to break him in a little at a time. If he proved to be a good man, then she would give him more and more responsibility. It would also give her a chance to see where he might need help, and then she could hire the people whom he suggested. The ranch was so large, she was sure Gonzales would ultimately need one or two assistant foremen just to direct his army of cowhands and a few people to keep track of the finances and other record books. Morgan sent for Julio again and asked him which women if any, had the skills she was looking for. There was only one. She did the bookkeeping and filed the reports that were sent to San Francisco.

The woman was summoned. She knew of two more women where she had gone to school; she was sure they would be glad to go to work for the Murdock ranch. Morgan smiled. The ranch was shaping up.

Later, she suggested they elect a mayor and a council to arbitrate problems that the ranch people might have among themselves. It was to be very like the town council, but dealing only with the ranch and ranch headquarters' non-business problems. In many ways the ranch's headquarters were larger than the town of Murdock, and all of the problems had more impact on the people there than anything that happened in town.

Like the town, the ranch was trashed and junky. Morgan's first order of business was to get it cleaned up. She called for hauling wagons and people to pick up the trash. The people came out of the woodwork. They were like ants; they seemed to want to clean up the visual blight and Morgan encouraged them. Instead of broken and rusted junk, she wanted flowers and shade trees and running water and flower boxes everywhere. The corrals were redesigned or relocated to include parts of streams and large shade trees so the horses could self-water and have shade. Water from the main stream was channeled through shallow ditches all around the headquarter buildings to irrigate the grass, trees and flowers. The water moistened the air and had a nice sound when it fell over rocks at the various small ripple falls.

Within ten days the ranch was a different place and the people took pride in being a part of it.

Cheyenne had taken out the fast guns, and the rest of the men shaped up. He didn't know who all of the Indian village raiders were, but he thought he had put a serious dent in their power bank. He was about to tell Morgan that he would soon be riding on to deal with his own loose ends, when a name came to his attention. A man from the Indian massacre showed up at the ranch looking for a job and got one.

Gonzales had hired a new man whose name was Jacobs. He was supposedly a friend of a friend. When Cheyenne heard the name Jacobs, he wondered if the man was the same person as one of the men still remaining on his list of renegades. Gonzales, the foreman, later pointed out Jacobs to Cheyenne and Cheyenne decided it was time to ask questions.

Jacobs had come there to hide. He knew nothing of Cheyenne, the avenger, nor did he know that anyone knew he was with the renegades when they attacked the Cheyenne Indian village.

Cheyenne could not be sure that this Jacobs was the same man he wanted, but he was a good judge of character and Jacobs looked to have spent much of his life hanging out under flat rocks. There was something crawly about the man. He asked Julio to have his people keep a sharp eye on Jacobs.

One of the last names on the list was Jacobs. A Jacobs shows up here at the Murdock ranch. It was too much of a coincidence. The ranch had been headless and disorganized and it was still very vulnerable and ripe for take over.

Morgan Murdock had fired many riders who were said to have been pals with the last foreman, some of whom were known "guns for hire" types. With their money well dried up, Cheyenne assumed, even though they were not on his list, those boys wouldn't take it lying down. He reasoned that they were confident they were still the best shooters around, and that they were probably forming a small army.

//////

"Yes, Cheyenne thought, they would attempt to take over the ranch, but how?" He reasoned that these villainous people could just move in, take out the few people in charge, and whip everyone else into shape through fear and intimidation, however, that wouldn't turn on the money supply. For that, they had to have control of Morgan Murdock. Cheyenne decided to stick to her like glue, to move before they did, and to get a small army of his own.

He decided not to wait. It was time to break heads. He asked Gonzales, the new ranch foreman, to pull his people away from the horse barns and then send the new man, Jacobs, to the barn tack-room to pick out his new riding equipment, ropes, saddle blankets, rain slicker, and other cowhand gear.

"Remember, Jacobs first."

As he headed for the barn he turned and said,

"You had better find a replacement for Jacobs and send someone to clean up after I've gone."

Gonzales raised an eyebrow and thought to himself, the boss lady has a very persuasive assistant.

Williams added further,

"Please ask Miss Murdock to saddle her horse and be ready to ride in ten minutes. Tell her it's important. Much obliged."

Gonzales thought to himself, with Cheyenne Williams' help, I could have the Murdock ranch running as smooth as a Swiss watch.

//////

When Jacobs arrived, Cheyenne pole axed him with his Colt. Jacobs dropped like a sack of rocks. He took Jacobs' gunbelt and his boots. Then he tossed a line over a rafter, put a clove hitch around Jacobs' ankles, another around his wrists, and tied his hands behind his back. When he did so, he noticed a small triangular tear in Jacob's blue shirt. The small piece of blue cloth in Cheyenne's pocket matched the hole in Jacobs' shirt. He had the right man. Jacobs was one of the raiders. Next he hoisted him up by his ankles, about five feet off the ground to hang up side down. He stripped off the man's shirt with the big knife and waited.

When Jacobs came around, the first thing he saw was that the world was up side down and a huge man was holding the biggest knife he had ever seen. He was in shock and stunned. When Jacobs could fully comprehend what was happening to him, Cheyenne split the man's left nostril with the point of the razor sharp blade. As the blood ran into his eyes, Williams asked,

"When do they plan to attack the ranch and how many men are involved?"

"You go to Hell."

Cheyenne swiftly made a horizontal cut across Jacobs' belly above his belt buckle, and deep enough to show the man some of his own blue-purple innards. Jacobs fainted.

Cheyenne threw water on him. When he revived, Cheyenne Williams said,

"You still have a chance to live. The next cut will spill your guts out onto the floor. You'll be dead and I'll find out what I want to know from Wainright, anyway."

Cheyenne held the huge blade vertically against Jacobs belly.

"All right, all right, for Chrisake." He yelled.

"Yeah, I rode with those men, so did Wainright. He was the leader. We're all that's left of that group. Something has happened to every one of those boys."

"I'm the something, that happened to everyone of those boys. Whose idea was it to raid the village?"

"Harnnaky. He hates redskins. He kills them whenever he gets the chance. His wife was taken by the Apache."

"Now, what about the Murdock ranch. How many people do you have at this time? And when do they plan to move on it?"

Jacobs replied through gritted teeth,

"Cut me down."

"I'll cut you down when you have answered all of my questions. So answer."

"So far, about twenty men and a few late arrivals. They will move on the ranch as soon as all of the men get here."

"When?"

He answered in short painful spurts, through clenched teeth.

"In about ten days. They're being met in town and shown the way out to the old line cabin in the pines, near that large southeast graze, until we're ready."

"Another surprise raid?"

"Yes," he whispered, through hurting everything. Jacobs was in severe pain.

"To kill everyone?"

"Yes."

"Just like the Indian village"

"Yes, yes. For God sake. Please cut me down."

"None of that is any good without money. I want the rest."

"We planned to grab the Murdock girl and hold her hostage."

Cheyenne thought while he paced. He had the information that he wanted. Very quickly he cut the rope. The resulting fall broke Jacobs' neck. Cheyenne was both ruthless and remorseless with vermin like him. He left Jacobs for Gonzales to feed to the vultures.

Minutes later Morgan arrived outside the barn with her own horse. She was met by Cheyenne and he steered her away from the grim carnage.

CHAPTER SIXTEEN

As soon as Cheyenne mounted, he and Morgan went for a ride. He felt the need to practice his knife throwing and told her so. They rode out toward a high-up aspen stand.

They had ridden into pretty country where they could see for miles. Off to the northeast they could see the rugged snow capped peaks of the Rocky Mountains. There was only a slight breeze, just enough to move the aspen leaves in their little wobbling dance. Away to the west, the vultures sailed across the sky and descended gracefully down in ever-smaller spirals. Cheyenne knew Gonzales' men had removed the dead men from the ranch headquarters area. He did not say anything to Morgan.

//////

They rode around a large area to be sure that they were alone and both dismounted. He ground tied his horse while she tied her black horse to a tree. Cheyenne began to practice by throwing his various knives at a large tree. After about thirty minutes, he felt as though he had "the touch" as he called it. He explained to Morgan about "the touch."

"The 'touch' is a kind of fine tuning of your own skill. It's when you know where the knife will strike before you throw it."

He had worked up a sweat. He retrieved his knives for the last time and examined their blade tips for any damage. He felt the presence of someone and looked up to see an Indian, far off, riding toward him. As he got closer, Cheyenne could see the man was not wearing war paint, but he was carrying a lance and astride a yellow pony. The Indian had one feather in his hair and there were two feathers fastened high on the tail of the pony. The pony had a handprint on his left flank. The handprint signified making coup against an enemy.

He cautioned Morgan to stand near the horses.

When closer, the Indian used both his voice, speaking in the Cheyenne Indian language, and sign language to say,

"I seek the one who is called, "Wims."

"I am the man they call Wims," Cheyenne said. Cheyenne was aware the man knew who he was, but he respected the ritual greeting. After a little more talk, the greeting was over, and they got down to business.

Cheyenne learned the name of the Indian was Shadowman and he had been sent to tell Wims of a plot by bad white men to take over the Murdock ranch. He also knew that Cheyenne single handedly had wrought vengeance upon most of the renegade group, which had wiped out the Cheyenne village of Chief Kua Tonta.

Shadowman told him the men buying gunmen to take over the Murdock ranch were the same ones that were on his list of remaining renegades.

Williams had not known the men he was looking for were the same men now threatening to take over the ranch, though he had suspected that some of them might be members of the village raid. They were all low life, guns for hire.

Shadowman had apparently been a day or two behind Cheyenne Williams all along the trail. It was he who had reported the slaughter of Kua Tonta's village to several other chiefs of the Cheyenne. The chiefs sent people to deal with the final remains of those killed during the village massacre.

It was in the interest of the Cheyenne tribes that the Murdock Ranch continued to operate just as it had in the days when Morgan's father was alive. The Indians could travel across the land, cut their lodge poles, hunt the land, and even have a steer now and then if they needed it. With the gradual demise of the buffalo, it was even more important that they get along with the management of the big spread. Neither did they want any more trouble with the blue coats. The Murdock people had treated them better than any of the other ranchers, at least, until lately.

The ranch foreman, Colby, was not above shooting Indians just for the fun of it. Now, it seemed that his pals were the major players in the threat to take over the Murdock ranch. The group had apparently been rustling cattle to sell to raise money to hire more gunmen to steal the entire ranch. If not for Cheyenne Williams and Shadowman, it might have worked.

How Shadowman learned all of this was not clear, but Cheyenne Williams believed him. These local Cheyenne were learning to pay attention to the white man's world for their own good. The Cheyenne Indians were also interested in reprisal against the renegades, as many of them were related to the people who died in the destroyed village. Shadowman had informed them of Cheyenne's efforts in that regard and they were very pleased and grateful.

The renegade raiders had gathered at a line cabin, three days ride from ranch headquarters. They planned to raid the farthest side of the ranch. They could gather cattle and sell them in a town that was several days drive from the Murdock ranch's northern most border at a place called, Dry Wells.

Cheyenne made a mental note to ask Spencer to look into the problem from his end, which meant leaning on the sheriff to see if any of the locals in Dry Wells were buying stolen cattle. Spencer could "spread some green" or send some of his hired cops, or both. It was important that the local officials feel some heat to realize honesty was the best policy where the big and powerful Murdock ranch was concerned.

It was a far piece from the ranch to anywhere and still farther to Dry Wells, but if it took the territorial governor to get the attention of the Dry Wells sheriff, then so be it. Spencer was very resourceful. He was also a big contributor to certain politicians, and he well knew the governor had a substantial force of rangers to help keep the peace in the region, to keep the town's citizens peaceful, and keep small town sheriffs reasonably honest. At the time, honesty was a virtue that was treated rather casually by more than a few small town sheriffs.

//////

Shadowman assured "Wims" that he would have all the help he needed to take out any of the village raiders who threatened the Murdock ranch. Pleased to hear this, Cheyenne asked Shadowman to place a "zillion" Indians around the line cabin, just out of rifle range. Then he gave him some good whiskey, a very good knife, thanked him, and said, "Good bye," and the Indian rode out.

Riding toward the ranch, Williams reasoned that without the help of Shadowman and the Cheyenne Indians, the rustlers could have operated for weeks with impunity and no one would have been the wiser. That was particularly true because Morgan had just appointed all new people to run things, and none of them had any idea of the situation of the ranch at that time. No one knew exactly where the cattle were, or how many they had, how many had wandered off the ranch, or even if any were stolen. There hadn't been a count that anyone could remember since Colby's arrival several years ago.

Cheyenne had noted on several occasions there were too many old cows, many yearling bulls, which should have been steers, and old bulls that should have been shipped. He had seen several animals that needed immediate attention, but that was the ranch foreman's problem. The cowhands would get to those problems in time.

//////

Cheyenne had his own problems. He was sure the raiders were busy recruiting a small army, even now. They could probably do it with promises. They would attempt to take Morgan prisoner. If they were successful in that endeavor, they would force her by threat, by pain, and by more serious tortures to sign checks until the money tree was dry. And it was conceivable, in this remote area, that they could keep her abduction a secret for some time.

Cheyenne decided it was time to crank up the people at the Murdock ranch. He sent word to Julio and Gonzales to meet him in the den of the main ranch house. When they arrived, he poured drinks for them and one for himself. When the men were comfortably seated and sipping their drinks, Cheyenne explained,

"Gonzales, I have reason to believe the disgruntled people Morgan fired are hiring guns to invade and take over this ranch."

He let that sink in and then continued.

"We must be prepared to keep them out. I would like for you and your men to turn this place into a fortress. If your people are placed well, we can send out a hail of lead that a squirrel couldn't get through."

"Gonzales, notify all of the cowhands to be on the lookout for trouble and issue guns to everyone."

"Julio, can you shoot or find someone to teach those who can't?"

"Si, I can give shooting lessons to anyone who needs them. At one time, I was a fair hand with one of these," and he pulled his own pistol, expertly spun it a few times and dropped it back into his holster.

Cheyenne smiled and continued,

"Post guards on all sides of the ranch headquarters on two-hour shifts for the next two weeks. Keep all strangers out, at gunpoint if you have to. Shoot them if necessary. Remember, no one gets in here for any reason, unless I say so. Hire new men, all of your own people, or anyone you're sure you can trust. Start building a sandbag wall, at least hip high, around the house and the barn, Keep a dozen of the best horses in the barn and rotate them so they stay fit. I want this place sealed up tight. Forget the cattle for a few days. Store extra food, water and ammo. Send riders to the outer camps and bring in as many men as you need to defend this place; at least fifty rifles. I don't believe those scoundrels will be ready to mount a war for a couple of weeks, but we can't be sure."

"Also, send a group of riders to intercept any people heading for the line cabin on that far north edge of the ranch. Do you know the cabin near the pine forest by the big graze?"

"Si, I know it."

"Catch or shoot anyone headed toward that cabin. We think those hired killers are making that cabin their headquarters. I want any stranger going there stopped. As I said, "Shoot if you have to."

"One more thing. I'm taking Miss Murdock away from here to a place where she will be safe. I will be back in about a week. You men have a big job on your hands. Keep your people sharp and do your best."

Gonzales spoke,

"Senor, you can count on all of us. Those pigs will not get in here."

Julio nodded in agreement.

The three men stood up, shook hands, and Cheyenne said,

"Good luck," and left.

CHAPTER SEVENTEEN

He found Morgan.

"Come on, girl, we're going for another ride."

They arrived at the town of Murdock after a long hard ride, and went straight to the telegraph office. Cheyenne had apprised Morgan of the problems. She wired Spencer to once again cut off all money to the ranch until he was contacted by Cheyenne. Spencer agreed to meet her in Denver in three days.

The two rested overnight in town, and the next day Cheyenne and Morgan boarded the train to Denver. With Spencer and his people she would be safely away from the Murdock ranch problems. He didn't intend to let her out of his sight until she was safely in the hands of Spencer and his army of hired, private detectives. When they arrived in Denver, they took rooms at one of the better hotels.

During the meeting, Cheyenne told Spencer how the Indians had first discovered the cow thieves and the plot to take over the Murdock ranch by all of the disgruntled ex-employees. Then he explained his plan to trap the villainous men at the cabin, using the hundreds of young Cheyenne braves at his disposal, to surround, isolate, intimidate and finally to starve the bad guys into coming out. He didn't tell Spencer that he planned as a reward for their help, to let the young Indian braves dispose of them.

He even told Spencer that it could probably be accomplished with a minimum of bloodshed. Of course, that meant different things to each of them.

Spencer, being a careful man with a buck, wanted to know what this was going to cost. Cheyenne answered,

"Perhaps a few beeves over the years for the Cheyenne Indians; more, if the buffalo are wiped out."

Spencer loved the idea of free labor from all of those Indians, and also free beef for them at little actual cost because he knew the bulls would be more than happy to do their part. He figured at present, the cows produced more cattle than the Indians would take, so he saw the deal as a win / win.

Spencer purred,

"Excellent, excellent. Why haven't we hired you before?"

Both men smiled and they shook hands. After the meeting and a pleasant dinner, Cheyenne and

Morgan left Spencer to count his money and retired to her room.

//////

The next morning Cheyenne took the train back to Murdock and coincidently happened to ride in the same car with two of the "bad guys." He heard them talking about the Murdock ranch being a soft job and ripe for the taking. Neither man ever arrived in Murdock and Cheyenne acquired two more six shooters.

The two men each did a header from a trestle high over a rocky ravine, and apparently, neither man was missed by anyone in the entire world. By the time Cheyenne arrived back in town both men had become vulture food.

In Murdock, Cheyenne walked to the stable to reclaim his obnoxious horse from the livery stable. The hostler immediately went into a lengthy diatribe about the brute. He said unkind things; called him, "crow-bait, boil him down to glue, he's got teeth like a mad wolf." He told how the nag knocked down two box-stall walls to get to a mare, and on and on. Cheyenne had heard it all before. He paid them for the trashed box stalls and a kicked through, outside wall, and saddled up. The hostler and his helper both said good riddance.

As he prepared to leave, Cheyenne said to the stable men,

"It's a good thing he was on his good behavior. You've still got a barn. If he had been in a real snorty mood, you would very likely just have kindling."

He loaded two pack mules with guns, ammo, food, and good scotch whiskey and headed for the Murdock ranch. As he left, the much abused horse hostler was still carrying on with his verbal harangue.

Cheyenne had been away eight days. Sometimes the great beast caused twice that much trouble, just overnight. The critter really had been on his best behavior. Williams, smiling to himself was sure the mare had something to do with it.

CHAPTER EIGHTEEN

When he arrived at the ranch, he found the place fortified and quiet. He met with Gonzales and Julio to have them bring him up to date. Then, he told them of the situation as he saw it. He told them of the Indians who were helping to contain the raiders, and that his plan was to starve the raiders out. For that to happen, he first had to get all of the cattle away from the area of the line cabin, at least beyond rifle range. That would be the sticky part. Cheyenne had some ideas to solve that problem, too. He then requested a small army of mounted riders who were reasonably good with guns to ride with him to reconnoiter the ranch. He wanted each man to be issued and to wear a yellow rain slicker, even if the sun was out. They would be gone several days.

Next, he wanted Julio to continue to keep a group of riders to intercept any of the village raiders thought to be headed toward the line cabin near the pine forest. The yellow raincoat interception committee must patrol from town, north as far as a six-hour ride and no further, so as not to run into the Indian guard.

The next day Williams and his army rode out at dawn toward the line cabin where the raiders were holed up. On the way, they chased and over-ran, three men who were headed for the cabin. The three men were shot to doll rags.

Days later, Cheyenne held up his hand for his riders to stop. They were in a small, well-concealed meadow, protected from the wind and watchful eyes. He explained, "From here on, I must go alone. It's about three miles to the line cabin. I am going to meet with several hundred Cheyenne warriors. I will tell them of your yellow raincoats. Do not take them off while you are anywhere near the line cabin because those warriors won't know you from the enemy. The warriors will be hunting hair, so wait here until I return. Stay sober."

Cheyenne Williams cantered the big stud horse along easily enough for a few miles until he met the first of several Cheyenne Indian out-riders. Soon they came to several tepees. Smoke was coming out of the smoke holes of the lodges. It was lunchtime. He shouted his greeting and many people came out of their lodges to meet him. The riders all dismounted, except for Cheyenne Williams. Leading their horses and escorting "Wims" the great warrior, they joined those who had come to greet him and walked back together. The people shouted “Wims. Wims. Wims.” The shouting was accompanied by a lot of smiles and much laughter.

He was asked to get down and enter the lodge of the main chief where other chiefs were present. Food was being served to the men by a few of the women.

After the men had eaten, the pipe was passed and smoked by all present, and then the discussion began. Wims told them of his blood-brother relationship to Chief Kua Tonta, and the chief’s brother, Kicks Hard. He spoke of the solemn pact made long ago, among the three of them. As members of the Wolf Society, each survivor was required to avenge the deaths of the others. It was his duty to take vengeance on the raiders of the village, and he had done that, except for the last man on the list, Wainright.

Cheyenne explained further that Wainright, who was the leader of the village raiders, was also, coincidentally, the leader of the new group who intended to take over the Murdock ranch. He further pointed out that none of those men were worthy of the attention of the tribes’ best warriors, but rather, it would be an opportunity for the young braves to take scalps. The old men nodded in assent.

Cheyenne continued to explain the situation and his plan for capturing and killing the raiders. He told them he had the word of the Murdock ranch people that conditions for all of the Cheyenne bands would be the same as they were when the Murdock chief was alive. They could use the land as always and cut their lodge poles in the same place as their ancestors had as always. They could cross the land freely and they could even continue to take a steer now and then, if they needed it for food. If the buffalo were there, they could continue to hunt them as always. The chiefs were very pleased with the conditions. The meeting was lengthy and solemn. They agreed to help and that Wims would be in charge.

Each chief offered his best young braves. When the total count of young warriors was known, the number staggered Cheyenne.

He thanked them and promised that they would all smoke the pipe again when the difficulty was over. He would bring whiskey so they could all celebrate together. The old men smiled and agreed. They were sure to the last man that this was how business should be done. Even Cheyenne Williams was proud of himself. He too, was sure that this was how business should be transacted.

Later, he met the young brave in charge of all of the other young Cheyenne. He liked the young fellow, and thought he had the stuff in him to one day become a chief. Cheyenne knew it would be difficult to restrain the young men, who of course wanted to take scalps immediately, but he advised that they wait so as not to lose any warriors.

He further explained that it was important for his own people, who would be wearing bright yellow rain slickers, to move all of the cattle away from the cabin in order to starve out the raiders. It wouldn't take long, as they were nearly out of food. In a few days when the raiders got hungry enough, they would come out and the young braves could have them. There was likely to be less risk to the Indians as the outlaws would be in a weakened condition. It was also probable that they would only come out a few at a time. The young brave was not at all sure that he could contain his men for that long a period. Cheyenne said,

"Those who are wise will wait."

"Umh!"

The two men rode away in different directions.

The young brave apprised his men that Cheyenne's men were all wearing bright yellow rain slickers. Then he posted roughly five hundred warriors around the cabin. Even out of rifle range, and ten feet apart, the warriors would still look like a solid wall around the line cabin.

The next morning the raiders were stunned. They had never seen so many hostiles. The equation had changed, and they were scared. By nightfall, many were planning to get the hell out of there, if they could. No ranch was worth losing their hair.

The first night, three men tried to get through the net. Three separate screams were heard and the next day three scalps were visible from three separate lances. Not a shot had been fired and none of the Cheyenne warriors were ever in any kind of danger. Arrows were silent. They were sure this was sly sport. They were already convinced that Wims was a great warrior, but now they were convinced that he was also a clever one and an equal to any chief as well.

With the first lesson taught, Wims decided to fire the grass near the cabin, hoping the smoke would obscure the cattle raid, and that it would help frighten the cattle away from the good grass around the line cabin. The scheme worked fine.

He sent several pairs of warriors crawling close enough to send flaming arrows at the grass around the cabin. He instructed them to light the arrows, shoot from upwind, quickly crawl away from that spot at least the length of four men, and then repeat the process.

In a short while he had all of the cows away from the cabin and had not lost a man. There was some shooting from the cabin, but no one was injured. Now, all he had to do was keep an eye on the raiders and starve them out. He figured three or four days ought to do it. He was right on all accounts. Each morning there were more scalps on more lances. Those boys who had heard Indians didn't fight at night discovered they had heard wrong.

Now, Cheyenne wanted Wainright. The problem was how to get him out of there alive. He figured there were at least a dozen men still remaining. He asked his Indian friends to wait for eight more days, knowing the raiders inside would be reduced nearly to cannibalism by that time. The Indians waited.

On the third day, some one in the cabin waved a flag of truce. Cheyenne chose to ignore it. That night, there were many more scalps on the lances of the young braves.

The following day, Cheyenne Williams asked for Wainright, but made no promises. The man was offered up immediately. The men in the cabin were all "bucked out" and they knew it. Surrendering to the yellow coats was better than being skewered for hours over a hot fire by a thousand angry Indian squaws.

Wainright rode toward Cheyenne Williams, his hands tied behind his back. Williams had four of his yellow rain slickers escort the man into his camp. He wanted to see the man who led the raid on Kua Tonta's village. He wanted to know why.

Wainright's answer was unsatisfactory so Wainright was turned over to the Cheyenne chiefs. It was for them to decide his fate. The remaining men in the cabin had joined the wrong side at a bad time and they knew it. They gave up, were disarmed, and given a choice: hanging or the Cheyenne squaws. They chose the hanging tree and were hanged by the men in yellow slickers. They thought it better than being given to the Cheyenne Indian squaws. They were right, of course. It was better, a whole lot better.

CHAPTER NINETEEN

Cheyenne rode back to the Murdock ranch with his army of yellow rain slickers and dismissed them. The hostilities were over. He was sure the word was out. Anyone who attacked the Murdock ranch would have to face a thousand Cheyenne warriors. Morgan's properties were intact and so was she. She didn't know it, but all of her enemies were under. It wasn't likely that anyone in that area would ever attempt such a thing again.

The party for the chiefs was a very big bash indeed. As promised, Cheyenne attended with two wagons loaded with booze and foods, and an army of Mexican cooks all wearing yellow rain coats to cook a small herd of fat steers. When they arrived, Cheyenne Williams gave a short speech.

"Anyone who causes trouble will have to clean up after the rest of us."

The Cheyenne people laughed and accepted that. The chiefs laughed at the yellow raincoats and agreed that it was probably a good idea. The chiefs had people monitor the flow of whiskey. The Cheyenne women laughed to see men roasting steers, but pitched in to help, and every one had a good time. After a while, the cooks were not so terrified. The party lasted two days. When it was over the leaders once again agreed that was how business should be transacted. Cheyenne Williams breathed a sigh of relief. His people still had all of their hair.

Cheyenne returned to the Murdock ranch with the wagons and his people. One or two had left some of their virtue back at the party, but not their scalps.

//////

Cheyenne's work was finished. He turned his horse toward the hills because he wanted to be alone in the high country where he could see far off into the distance. When he got there, he discovered that he was really looking inside himself.

Two days later he rode toward the Cheyenne Indian lodges. The Cheyenne were so pleased with Wims' solution to the problem and his vengeance on the raiders of the village that they bestowed upon him another eagle feather, and the benefits that went with such an honor.

They were particularly pleased that none of their young braves were injured, and there would be no keening by the women, no scarring, no cutting off of fingers, no pulling of the hair, and no covering themselves with ash by the squaws. On the contrary, the single squaws were practically standing in line to reward their returning heroes, and so were some of the married ones. They probably would have been standing in line to reward Cheyenne Williams even if he had lost every man jack of them. Cheyenne was an especially attractive man and they all were well aware of it. A fortunate few were very much aware of his masculine charms. In fact, he favored a few of these dusky damsels, just for old times sake, before he rode off to the world of the white man and Morgan Murdock. After all, he had promised himself a bonus and he was well aware that a bonus might arrive in any kind of package. It did, several and similar.

THE END

EPILOGUE

Cheyenne rode to town to send a wire to Spencer.

He wrote, "Problem solved. Morgan can come home when she wishes. Am sending big bill for whisky party with Cheyenne chiefs.

Suggest Morgan remain Denver until I get there."
She did and he did.

Then they both did.

//////

Williams was sprawled in a chair with a big glass of scotch. He was watching the color and the light swirl around inside the glass.

Across the room, Morgan Murdock was purring and watching him.

She said,

"A million dollars for your thoughts."

He gave her a serious contemplative look and said,

"Vengeance leaves scars."

"Yes, I know," she offered, "I'm here to help you heal yours."

Cheyenne smiled.

THE END